A COUPLE OF THOU

Upon starting a new job, you never know who y
can do is hope to roll a six and that you will, at least
colleagues.

The beauty of working in the world of retail is that the doors of your shop are a
portal where anyone from all walks of life can enter, and either make or break your
day.

Copyright © Tom Neath 2018
All Rights Reserved

CONTENTS

Copyright © Tom Neath 2018
All Rights Reserved

INTRODUCTION

My inspiration to write this book began with an experience while job hunting in winter 2001. It was my second visit of the week to Broadmead (Bristol's main shopping centre), in the hope of finding a suitable vacancy that had full-time hours. After my second lap around the shops, without spotting anything vaguely suitable and the gloomy weather matching my mood, I decided to bring an end to the day's job hunting proceedings and catch the bus home. As my bus pulled up to the stop, I noticed someone putting up a sign outside a camping and clothing shop which read 'full time staff wanted'. Bingo!

Eager to find out more about the role, I went into the shop and I saw a man dressed in full ski-wear - jacket, salopettes, gloves, goggles and helmet - displaying some highly erratic ski moves! I noticed a member of staff by the cash desk, approached him.

"You had better tell your manager that you have a madman in the store!" I said.

"That is the manager, sir!!! He's product testing." the member of staff replied.

Upon hearing my interest in the advertised position, the manager, still in full ski-wear, wanders over and Informs me about the role. He ended his introduction by bellowing *"The pay is awful, but the entertainment is great!"*

Undeterred by the awful pay, as it would still be a lot more than the 'wage' from the job centre, I took an application form. As I was leaving the shop the manager added *"you don't have to be mad to work here, but it helps!"*

After completing a successful application process with the camping and outdoor clothing shop, my retail career in Broadmead had begun.

Copyright © Tom Neath 2018
All Rights Reserved

WELCOME TO BROADMEAD

Before I share my stories with you, let me paint a picture of Broadmead Shopping Centre. On the face of it, it has the same appearance as any other shopping centre - busy shops, quiet shops, budget shops, top brand shops and the choice of a thousand eateries. Joining these familiar sights are the *100-miles-per-hour-shoppers*, as I call them, dashing around in search of the latest 'must have' product, fighting their way past the casually strolling browser, themselves in search of a bargain. But, as I have visited a lot of shopping centres around the country, Broadmead is certainly unique, as it is the characters that I have worked with and served that have made this place such a memorable place to work, though not always for the right reasons! Throughout the years, these characters have ranged from the weird to the wonderful, the cheerful to the moody, and the humorous to the, well, not quite so humorous!

Upon entering the busy world of Bristol's top shopping location, the first thing that you hear and see, sat outside a well-known department store, is a homeless flute-playing fellow. Not a particularly talented flute player, mind you, as he played the same ten seconds in a nine hour loop! But due to his social position, I could forgive him for giving my ears some grievous bodily harm! If this fellow did know how to play a selection of tunes, and he wanted to give them names that were reminiscent of Broadmead, I'm sure that he would entitle the album *"Blowing Down The Mead"* *(Now That's What I Call Flute Music!)* featuring the hit songs *"Spare Some Change Governor?"*, *"Where Is The Nearest Mobile Phone Shop?"* and the European smash hit *"Mum, I Want A Burger!!!"*

So upon my first day of work at the camping and outdoor clothing shop, I have put my first take of an early morning in Broadmead in the form of a short poem-

The just opening bakery,
Providing a heart-warming essence.
For retailers and customers,
Upon their Broadmead entrance.
Mature Murray minters,
Reminiscing about the past and present.

Copyright © Tom Neath 2018
All Rights Reserved

Joined by the happy go lucky bin men,

That keep the streets of Broadmead clean and pleasant.

The seagulls and tramps,

Desperate in their search for feed.

But with the hand of pity from the city's folk,

They will succeed.

Yuppies speeding their way to work,

Wearing sunglasses and spray tanned.

But how cool can you really be,

Cruising past Poundland?!

Just a few shops down from the flute player was my place of employment - the camping and outdoor clothing shop. The shop was part of a small family run business, with twenty five other shops and head office making up the company. The company had been in existence for a long time and up until very recently, had been in good financial health.

As well as selling ski-wear and accessories (so elegantly modelled by the shop manager!), the shop sold everything for a really successful camping trip – tents, rucksacks, sleeping bags, walking boots, waterproof clothing. In fact, if you got an hour to spare - only joking! I am not going to sit here and list every item that the shop stocked, as there are a lot of nominations! In fact, the only camping accessory that the shop did not stock was a ready-made, lit, camp fire! (This was actually a genuine customer request, I kid you not folks!) The company never attempted to compete with the bigger names in the camping and outdoor clothing industry, and the stock was made up of modest brands set at the low to middle price range, was of good quality and popular with our customers.

Right, that's enough *rambling* about the setting (pardon the pun!) Let's crack on with the stories! So to my first shift.

Copyright © Tom Neath 2018
All Rights Reserved

A LEARNING CURVE

Come on in and meet the Manager Mr. G and the Assistant Manager Mr. S! No, they are not the arch enemies of a well-known fictional spy, but due to legal issues, this is how I will refer to them and other work colleagues throughout the book. (This was due to the advice from my lawyer who is currently on holiday in the Costa Del Sol. It's been one long holiday, as he has been there for five years.)

Mr.G and Mr.S were remarkably similar in appearance - same height, crew cut hair and a stocky build - but that is where the similarities end! With regards to personality they were a million miles apart. Mr.G was an eccentric nymphomaniac that took great pleasure in comical impressions and dancing around the shop. Well, comical to some, annoying to others. Mr.S was one of the others! Mr.S was highly skilled and professional at his job, hardworking and could not abide people of an eccentric nature and those fond of a sexual innuendo or two! So in a nut shell, Mr.S took a professional and personal dislike to Mr.G's antics.

So let's start with an example of Mr.G doing what he does best - winding up Mr.S. Being new, not just to retail but also to the world of work, I had the mentality of simply 'do as you are told', and in doing this I unwittingly helped Mr.G kick off another day of antics designed to wind up Mr.S.

"Right then lad",' bellowed Mr.G in the tone of a Sergeant major, *"your first task of the day is to test every whistle in that tray, making sure that they are all in working order".*

I turned to the cash desk where over one hundred, fifty pence whistles lay in a tray. I had better get cracking!!! I picked up a whistle and blew-'FWEEEEEEEEEEEEEEEEEEEP' I picked up another whistle and blew-'FWEEEEEEEEEEEEEEEEEEEP' I picked up another whistle, and just as Mr.S was about to speak - 'FWEEEEEEEEEEEEEEEEEEEEEEEEEEEEEEP!!!'

"THAT'S ENOUGH!" barked Mr.S. *"This is just a little joke that Mr.G plays on new members staff."*

I turned to see Mr.G sniggering away to himself. A joke?! How hilarious, I sarcastically thought to myself. Did I further embarrass myself on my first day? You bet!

Mr.S introduced me to the signing in book.

Copyright © Tom Neath 2018
All Rights Reserved

"Who signs it?" I asked enthusiastically.

"Anyone that visits the shop that is not a company employee" replies Mr.S.

With that, I spotted a customer browsing at the back of the shop, so I grabbed the signing in book and dashed to the back of the shop! Mr.S blocked my path and asked what on earth I was doing?! I told him that I have spotted someone that is not with the company - he needs to sign in!!! Mr.S snatched the signing in book out of my clutches, sighed and said that we don't ask customers to follow this course of action! Ooops.

My last error of the day centred on a soldier and his attractive girlfriend. The couple had spent a few minutes looking at the sock selection, chose a pair to purchase and approached myself at the cash desk. Now this guy was huge - he made Arnold Schwarzenegger look tiny! Not only this, but he was a good looking guy that had a charming aura, of which his girlfriend truly adored. As I was processing their payment I foolishly decided to try and impress the couple.

"I've just joined the gym, so I'm going to have huge muscles just like you."

The soldier triumphantly replied that he has great muscles because he is in the army, as his girlfriend looked over his impressive physique. Determined to impress, I continued *"I'm in the army too! They begged me to join!"*

The soldier, not believing me for one second, asked me out of politeness what regiment I was with. Regiment? I was stunned, what is a regiment?! The only response I could muster was, England!!! The couple smiled, took their purchase and left the shop. Oh dear.

So after my first day of work, I had learned three valuable lessons.

1. Do not believe everything that your manager says;
2. Be yourself; and
3. The customers do not have to sign in!!!

Copyright © Tom Neath 2018
All Rights Reserved

A SIGHT FOR SORE EYES

As previously mentioned, one of Mr.G's personality traits was that he was a nymphomaniac - and a professional one at that! He was very quick to let his fellow members of staff know that a pretty woman was walking past the shop, or that there is a 'cracking' new weather presenter on the television set. These, and similar comments, occurred frequently throughout the day, every day. The only way Mr.S could deal with the antics was to walk away and make a cup of tea. He got through twenty cups a day! Needless to say that Mr.G likes nothing more than when a customer shares the same philosophy.

It was a typical quiet Monday morning in early 2002 and a smart suited gentleman in his early fifties entered the shop and approached Mr.S at the cash desk.

"Good morning, how can I help?" asks Mr.S.

The gentleman inquired as to whether we sold binoculars and Mr.S began the sales patter.

"Certainly sir, I have a fantastic pair for you, they have 10x25 vision, tinted lenses and comes in a protective carry case, all for the great price of...", but before he could finish, the customer said,

"IS IT STRONG ENOUGH TO SEE INTO MY NEIGHBOURS BEDROOM WINDOW?"

Mr.S dropped the binoculars in shock at such a question!

At this point, Mr.G bulldozed his way into the conversation.

"Oh yes, they are definitely strong enough to see into the neighbours window!"

Mr.S was more than happy to step aside and let Mr.G take over the sale.

"Yes, that looks just the ticket, I'll take two pairs please" said the gentleman.

"Two pairs eh? I suppose the other pair is a present?" asks Mr.G.

The gentleman continued *"No, the other pair is to keep in my office drawer, I work opposite the Bristol Royal Infirmary and well, some of those nurses..."*

To which Mr.G replies, in an excitable yet slightly jealous tone, *"OH, I KNOW WHAT YOU MEAN, YOU LUCKY DEVIL!!!"*

The gentleman paid for his goods and asked if we also sold cameras. On a very rare occasion where Mr.S lacked his professionalism, he barked out

"NO, WE DON'T SELL CAMERA'S!"

Copyright © Tom Neath 2018
All Rights Reserved

Although the gentleman did not specify why he wanted a camera, it does not take a genius to work out that the camera would also have been put in his office drawer next to the binoculars, both rearing their ugly heads as each pretty nurse enters or exits their place of work. At this point Mr.S, understandably, had had enough of Mr.G's newly formed pact with the gentleman and stormed off to make his de-stressing cup of tea. The gentleman left the shop with Mr.G beaming.

"Well, that's my kind of customer" he quipped! What, a pervert?! I thought to myself.

Thankfully the perverted customers that entered the shop were few and far between, but perhaps that is because they were all sat outside the Bristol Royal Infirmary.

Copyright © Tom Neath 2018
All Rights Reserved

ON YOUR BIKE: PART 1

In this next story Mr.G was playing with fire. One morning in the summer of 2003, Mr.S, a devoted cyclist, had arrived for work with a brand new bicycle and took great pride in showing it off to myself and Mr.G. Now, I am no expert on the technical aspects of modern bicycles (I am still using my great Granddad's penny farthing as a mode of transport!), but I could tell that this was one quality bicycle that had put a severe dent in Mr.S's bank balance! Mr.S had stationed his prized asset in the yard behind the shop and it was certainly safe from theft, as he had not one, but three locks!

Mr.G had been strangely subdued throughout the day, meaning Mr.S was stress free - making just one routine cup of tea on his lunch break. But boy this was about to change! It was the end of the day, the last customers had trickled out of the shop and it was time to close. Mr.G was finishing cashing up the till and Mr.S went to the back yard to get his bicycle.

Shortly after, the door at the back of the shop swings open causing an almighty bang, and standing in the doorway, holding his bicycle is Mr.S - with a face like thunder! As he approached myself and Mr.G, I could see that his bicycle had undergone a facelift! Attached by string to the back of the bicycle was empty food tins, and attached to the front was a 'JUST MARRIED' sign!

"WHO IN THE FUCKING HELL HAS DONE THIS TO MY BIKE?!" screams Mr.S.

"Ah! The happy couple!" announces Mr.G.

Mr.G then throws a handful of ripped up pieces paper over Mr.S and his bicycle - creating a confetti effect!!

"I just want to wish you and your new love all the very best for the future" Mr.G continues. I swear that if looks could kill, Mr.S would have killed his nemesis ten times over!

Mr.S then demanded a pair of scissors to rid his bike of its decorations. Mr G then delivered a fatal blow to Mr.S's hopes of travelling home free of embarrassment.

"Sorry, I broke the scissors earlier and threw them out!"

The shop was out of stock of Swiss army knives, so Mr.S had no way of removing the decorations unless he wanted to chance damaging his prized asset. In hindsight, maybe it was for the best that the shop *was* out of stock of Swiss army knives, as I

Copyright © Tom Neath 2018
All Rights Reserved

am not one hundred per cent convinced that Mr.S would have used one for *just* sorting his bike out! He then took a deep breath and informed Mr.G that if he finds out that the bike has been damaged in any way, shape or form, then he would be paying for the repairs. He then exits the shop, hops on his bicycle and rides off in to the evening - with the sound of clattering tin cans engulfing the ears of myself and Mr.G!

I could no longer hold the laughter in! Yes, the act was a little naughty, but at the end of the day, the bike was not damaged and it provided a bit of light relief after a mundane shift. As I was getting my belongings from the staffroom I noticed, shoved behind a cupboard, the 'broken' pair of scissors and that they had miraculously fixed themselves! To avoid the chance of Mr.S finding them and making the situation worse, I decided to throw them out - exactly as Mr.S was told. Tut tut Mr.G!

Unfortunately for Mr.S, this was not the only time that Mr.G would use his bicycle to push his stress levels through the roof.

Copyright © Tom Neath 2018
All Rights Reserved

THE FASHION CONCIOUS TRAMP

Every year the shop held a fancy dress day to raise funds for a charity of head office's choosing, of which all staff participated in. There was, of course, a small fee for wearing fancy dress, but this also went to the selected charity.

Autumn 2003 saw my first participation in these events and I asked head office if the proceeds could go to the 'Tom Neath lager fund!' Unfortunately this was declined, but was at least taken in the good humour that it was intended. Mr.G was absent from this event, so it was myself, Mr.S and a young female assistant running the show. The female assistant came elegantly dressed as Marilyn Monroe (boy, did I search long and hard for a street vent to replicate the dress blowing scene from 'The Seven Year Itch!'). Mr.S sported a black curly wig and adopted the 'rock star' look. As I was told by Mr.S that a 'birthday suit' is not an actual item clothing, I adopted the 'surfer dude' look, which consisted of a floral Hawaiian shirt, Bermuda shorts and trendy red beach shoes.

It had been a busy morning – we had already hit our sales target for the day and the customers were digging deep in to their pockets to help fill the charity bucket. Mr.S, the female assistant and I were taking a well-deserved breather when an old homeless man, in stereotypical attire, enters the shop. He shuffles over to myself, points at my red footwear and started laughing! He then tells me that I shouldn't wear red shoes, especially with the shirt that I was wearing! I could not believe what was happening here - I WAS BEING GIVEN FASHION ADVICE BY A TRAMP!!! He then said that he wanted to buy a small gas cartridge for his cooker.

"I have been living on the streets since the 1960's and I have been using the same cooker for all that time" the homeless man stated proudly.

I processed his payment for the gas cartridge and he inquired as to why we were all in fancy dress. I told the man that it was the company's annual fund raising event. He then asks *"where is the collection pot?"*

Now, this gentleman was not very mobile, so with the chances of a snatch and run virtually non-existent, I pointed to wear the collection bucket was located. He then shuffles his way over to the bucket and paused. What on earth is he up to? Then one of those moments occurred that made me ask myself if I was in the middle of a Monty Python sketch! The man pulled out a huge handful of loose change, at

Copyright © Tom Neath 2018
All Rights Reserved

least £20 worth by my reckoning, and tipped every last coin in to the collection bucket!!! He then shuffles out of the shop to continue, I presume, his daily routine of begging on the streets of Broadmead. Now, I am as sure as I can be that this man was being truthful and that he was indeed living on the streets - you tend to know if a person is genuinely homeless or not. But in saying that, how many homeless people do you see giving over twenty pounds to charity?!

The day was a roaring success - we comfortably beat our daily sales target and the shop had made over £150 for charity. We told head office the good news and inquired to what charity the money was going to, to which the answer was, a charity for the homeless!!!

Copyright © Tom Neath 2018
All Rights Reserved

USE YOUR LOAF!

After this story, like myself, you will never again think of the phrase 'use your loaf' in the 'to use one's common sense' way it was intended, I guarantee!

Going back to my first week with the shop, I had just returned from my lunch break and Mr.G and Mr.S were going over some paper work at the cash desk. Mr.G asked myself, in the tone of a Sergeant Major,

"Are you back from your lunch break now lad?" to which I replied that I was and asked why he adopts the military tone of voice. Mr.G replied that he used to serve in the army. GREAT! Were there about to be a string of hair raising tales of how heroic he was? No chance! He further informed me that all he did in the army was play the triangle in the regimental band!!! Oh, the phrases involving the words 'damp squid' and 'lead balloon!' come to mind. I asked why he had left the army and he replied that the simple reason was he had gone as far as he wanted to go with the forces and wanted a return to civvy street. I was being a right old nosey parker, as I continued the interrogation.

"Did you come straight to work here from leaving the army?"

Mr.S jokingly asked if I was a policeman, before Mr.G replying,

"After leaving the army I went to work for a well-known sex shop".

I guess that could explain his obsession with the opposite sex!

Now, I would have thought Mr.G working for a well-known sex shop would have gone hand in hand, so naturally I inquired why he had left the sex shop.

"I hated having to deal with the returned products and I got caught product testing."

Despite being very quick to remove a very disturbing image from my mind, I wondered how deeply mentally scarred I would be from this conversation!

Mr.G continued, *"don't look so concerned, I used to check that the erotic videos were in working order, from start to finish!"*

So basically Mr.G was sacked from the sex shop because of watching porn films all day!!!

Mr.G said that he had watched some very entertaining films and strongly recommended that I should consider purchasing some titles!

"YOU DON'T KNOW WHAT YOU'RE MISSING!" he bellowed.

Copyright © Tom Neath 2018
All Rights Reserved

I replied that I couldn't watch any films of that nature, even if I wanted to, as my video player was broken. Mr.G responded,

"Well I managed perfectly well for years until I got my first video cassette player, because of this little tip that I'm going to share with you that I picked up in my teens."

Mr.S looked up from the paper work and asked if 'this little tip' was suitable for the shop floor? Mr.G showed complete ignorance to Mr.S, and continued.

'If you don't have access to a video player or it is broken, and you get a sudden urge to enjoy yourself, what you want to do is this- pop up on the wall a picture of the woman that you most desire. Then, get a loaf of bread, dig out a hole...'

"How big?" I asked.

Mr.G winked and said *"that depends on how lucky you are! Then pop it in the microwave for half a minute then voila! Enjoy yourself!"*

I looked up from my note taking to observe Mr.S looking to the heavens for help! Oh, that was not the end of the tip folks! Mr.G continued.

"The first time I tried this I made the mistake of buying a sliced loaf for the purpose!"

"Oh, not that old chestnut" sarcastically commented Mr.S!

"But the second time I tried it, boy did I learn" triumphantly announces Mr.G!

"Not only did I buy an unsliced loaf, I got one with nuts and seeds for extra pleasure!!!"

After composing myself from a fit of laughter, I glanced over to see Mr.S with a look as if to say 'get me the number of the Samaritans!', but thankfully for Mr.S, Mr.G muttered the words that guarantees at least one daily smile from Mr.S – *"I'm going on my lunch break!"*

I asked Mr.S if he had heard this pearl of wisdom before, to which Mr.S exclaimed,

"NO, ODDLY ENOUGH I HAVE NEVER BEEN ADVISED BY MANAGER TO STICK MY PENIS IN A LOAF OF BREAD!!!"

Just for the record this was a tip that I have not put into practice, or ever will put into practice! Mr.G folks, keeping bakeries going since 1969!!!

Copyright © Tom Neath 2018
All Rights Reserved

ONE IN A MILLION

During my time working for the camping shop, I have worked with a heck of a lot of different people, ranging from the good to the bad, (there are a few contenders for 'the ugly' too!) The next person I would like to introduce you to is most certainly in the 'good' category, so please put your hands together and give it up for K.T! WOOP WOOP! To say that I was fond of her is the understatement of the century. She was similar in appearance to the beautiful film actress Audrey Hepburn, had a terrific sense of humour and we 'clicked' from day one.

K.T joined us in early 2006, after being informed that her previous employers would be cutting her hours down. Their loss was certainly our gain! She had completed all the Duke Of Edinburgh challenges (an award scheme for youngsters with challenges set in the great outdoors), so she came armed with a good level of knowledge of outdoor clothing and equipment. Within an hour of her first shift she had made a witty comment that superbly summed up the vast range of products that we stocked. K.T was having a telephone conversation with a customer talking about the boil in the bag foods.

"Yes sir, we currently have the beans and sausages, beef stew and dumplings and jam roll and custard in stock. Yes I can reserve you one of each. Yes, we also sell jackets that have a hydrostatic head of up to 5,000 millilitres, an interactive zip and a structured hood"

K.T then has a chuckle to herself, which is overheard by her customer on the other end of the telephone.

"Oh sorry about the laughter" K.T continues, *"It's just that I swear that this is the only shop in the world where I can talk about high specification jackets AND beans, dumplings and jam roly poly in the same sales conversation!!!"*

Brilliant.

During my time working with K.T I had sensed that she had gone through a deep trauma or heartache at some point in her life, and one morning in early 2010, where she had not been her bubbly self, I decided to ask her what was wrong. She stared at me for a few seconds, then she was about to say something.

Copyright © Tom Neath 2018
All Rights Reserved

"EXCUSE ME, I NEED SOME HELP RIGHT THIS INSTANCE!!!" bellowed a posh middle aged lady looking at our selection of footwear. K.T went to assist the lady using her wonderful charm and personality that I had grown very fond of.

"How I can help?" K.T politely asked the lady. The lady snapped back that she was in a rush, as she is parked on double yellow lines (yes. in such a rush that she spent a good fifteen minutes mooching around the shop and had earlier declined Mr.S's offer of assistance!) The lady than asked why a certain sandal was so expensive, to which K.T replied,

"You should see the price of the left sandal!"

The lady moaned *"it's a scandal"*.

A sandal scandal I thought to myself!

The lady continued *"I'm not interested in sandals anyway, it is ladies winter garments I would like to see."*

K.T invited the lady to accompany her over to the ladies garments and the lady snaps.

"I CAN SEE WHERE THEY ARE! IF I NEED YOU I WILL WAVE"

Then, with a hand gesture, the lady shoos K.T away! Cheeky cow! Credit to K.T, she has the patience of saint. By my reckoning even Mother Teresa would have told this lady to piss off by now! I had the feeling that we had not heard the last of from the lady and her spiteful ways and I was not wrong.

After half an hour, the lady had selected 1,264 garments to try on. Ok, that is a little exaggeration folks, but she selected a heck of a lot of garments, considering she was in such a rush! After an hour of the lady being camped in the changing room (pardon the pun!), she emerged sporting one of our grey waterproof jackets and waved out to K.T for assistance. K.T took a deep breath and approached the lady. In a rather demanding voice, the lady asks,

"Thank you for making the time to assist, now tell me, does this coat suit me?"

K.T replies *"Well darling, the colour matches your hair!"*

"I BEG YOUR PARDON?" the lady snapped.

"I said it looks good to be fair!" KT replied.

The lady said that she would like to purchase the coat and then, she has the cheek to inquire as to whether there is a special discount for the more mature lady! In another quick and clever reply K.T informed the lady that there is no discount for the 'more mature lady' but there was an additional charge for the rude elder lady!!!

Copyright © Tom Neath 2018
All Rights Reserved

As K.T was processing the lady's payment, the lady moaned that wherever she goes, she always gets treated 'appallingly' by shop staff. K.T, being more constructive than rude.

"Well maybe there is a message in that?!"

The lady huffed, snatched her purchase away from K.T, who just put the garment neatly in a bag, and storms off to towards the shop doors. As she exits the shop, the alarm system is activated. K.T approaches the lady and explains that there is security tag left on the garment and apologises.

"Well sort it out quickly will you!" orders the lady.

K.T took out the security tag, hands the purchase back to the lady and politely informs the lady that if we were fortunate enough to be treated again to her presence, then it would be appreciated if she would have the decency to treat the staff with a little more respect. A perfectly reasonable request, right? The lady, with her nose severely put out of joint, bellows.

"WELL I NEVER! THIS IS THE MOST APALLING SERVICE I HAVE EVER RECIEVED! I DEMAND A REFUND RIGHT THIS INSTANCE!"

K.T informs the lady that this would not be a good idea and points to the lady's car parked on double yellow lines. The lady turns, has a face of horror and darts out of the shop shouting.

"OH DAMN AND BLAST! WARDEN! WARDEN!"

While putting the mountain of garments that the lady tried on back on to their hangers, I said to K.T that I thought I saw her take a security tag out of the garment while processing the lady's payment. K.T said that she did take a tag out and then she spotted a traffic warden walking towards the lady's car! So in effort to hold the lady up, and for her car to be noticed by the traffic warden, she put the loose security tag back into the lady's carrier bag! Not the nicest of actions, but justified I feel, as the lady was not the nicest of customers! K.T continued,

"I know she is a paying customer, but is that a reason for treating shop staff worse than something you find on the sole of your shoe?"

K.T wanted to work in musical theatre, in the glamorous surroundings of London's West End and she certainly had the talent and drive to achieve this. Shortly after the previously mentioned incident, she moved to the 'big smoke' to live her dream. I do not mind admitting that after my last shift with K.T, I shed more than a tear and I indulged myself in a quite a few lagers that night in my local pub. At one point that

Copyright © Tom Neath 2018
All Rights Reserved

night the juke box had jammed on the Bill Withers hit song 'Ain't No Sunshine', repeating itself six times in a row! I swear that this was beyond a coincidence.

I never did find out about her trauma or heartache, but I hope that she is enjoying success and most importantly, she is happy.

Copyright © Tom Neath 2018
All Rights Reserved

MR.G PUTS HIS FOOT IN IT AGAIN. AGAIN. AND AGAIN!

Mr.G always likes to be the entertainer, the one that gets the laughs. In his mission to get a laugh from staff members and customers alike, he would often step into the offensive field and his comments were often in earshot of the intended target! How he did not have a list of complaints as long as his arm made against him, I will never know! So without further ado, here is a selection of his comments to make you shuffle a little uncomfortably in your seat.

Customer: Do you have anything to hold cameras?
Mr.G: Yes, my hands!

Customer: Where are your walking socks?
Mr.G: On my feet!

Customer: You do not stock my required brand of foot liner, which is not very good is it?
Mr.G: Put a sock in it!

Customer: Can you help me please, I am on a wild goose chase!
Mr.G: Sorry madam, we do not stock wild geese!

Ok, those were severely watered down examples, but now try downing these without shuddering.

This next customer regularly came into store and spent an eternity browsing before deciding upon an item of stock to purchase. On this occasion, the customer was holding a pair of trousers size 34 long and approached Mr.G

Customer: Defy *long* for me
Mr.G: Ok. Long- the amount of time that you spend in here before making a purchase!

Customer: I must be dumb, as I am having trouble understanding this product.
Mr.G: Yes.

Customer: You are not supposed to agree with me!
Mr.G: But the customer is always right!!!

Copyright © Tom Neath 2018
All Rights Reserved

A perfectly polite female customer, with a tomboy appearance, selected some thermal wear to purchase.

> Customer: These will keep me nice and warm for the rugby!
> Mr.G: What position do you play?!

A customer who did not have a lot going on in the looks department, was about to make a purchase and slots his bankcard into the card machine, then Mr.G says,

"The card machine will ask you for your number. I bet that you are not used to being asked for your number!"

A large lady customer, comfortably in the 24-28 size bracket enters the shop.

> Customer: Do you sell anything that will fit me?
> Mr.G: Well, we sell tents!

Another large lady customer enters the shop, holding a 'The Body Shop' bag. Mr.G observes this, turns to me and says.

"I hope that the body she has in the bag is a damn sight more pretty than her current one!"

Tut tut Mr.G! His own staff could not escape his devilish tongue lashings either.

A customer wanders in to the shop and approaches Mr.S.

> Customer: Hello, I need some help acquiring some products, but I know nothing about camping and walking!
> Mr.G: Ah! You have something in common with Mr.S. as he does not know anything about camping and walking either!

It was the birthday of a female assistant and we were in conversation about her forthcoming night on the town

Copyright © Tom Neath 2018
All Rights Reserved

Me: (to the female assistant, in jest) Don't drink too much tonight, otherwise you will be dancing on the tables and end up stripping!

Mr.G: Yes, like she does in her other job!

But the devilish tongue lashings became a lot less frequent after a dramatic turning of the tables. With a queue of customers waiting impatiently to pay for their goods, I was rooted to the cash desk, working my backside off to reduce the queue as quickly as possible. Mr.G had returned to the shop from picking up his lunch and announced that he would be in the staff room if he was needed. (As there was only one cash till, an extra member of staff would not really have been that much more beneficial!)

Customer: Why on earth would he need you? Don't let your pasty go cold you horrible interfering old toad!

As the customers in the queue giggled away to themselves, Mr.G was as embarrassed, as he was stunned. I don't think he knew whether to laugh or cry! He was going to retaliate until he realised who the customer's companion was - none other than Bristol based, five time boxing world champion Jane Couch! Although the customer that had ridiculed Mr.G looked menacing enough, I am sure that it was the sight of Ms. Couch that prompted Mr.G to back down and scuttle off to the staffroom to devour his pasty!

So, it does seem that what goes around, does indeed come around!

Copyright © Tom Neath 2018
All Rights Reserved

TOO MUCH CHOICE

The above title means exactly what it says - there is simply too much choice these days. Walk into any supermarket and you will come across over fifty types of butter or fifty types of bottled water! In my shop it is no different. Now don't get me wrong, I am all for a healthy selection of stock, but I ask you - is there really a genuine need for fifty types of fleece jacket or fifty styles of ski glove?! No is the correct answer, and now for the chance to win tonight's star prize! Can you tell me why there is so much choice? No? Ok I will tell you. It is simply because that over the last ten years or so a lot of brands have tried to break into the already crammed outdoor clothing and equipment market (not to mention my crammed shop!) by offering their goods to the retailers at prices simply too good to turn down. Then before you know it, the shop has sixty varieties of sock to go with the sixty pairs of sock already being stocked!

I will be honest, and not so modest - my stock knowledge is at a very good standard, but if a customer wants to know the difference between two different brands of sun hat that look identical, have the same technical specifications (though how many technical specifications can a £4.99 sun hat really have?!), but there is a one pound price difference, I'm damned if I can tell the customer the difference!

If there was less choice to boggle the customer's minds, then it would be a lot easier for the customer to make a decision between products, instead of my hearing being constantly battered by the line that killed a thousand sales...

"I MAY BE BACK!!!" I rest my case.

Copyright © Tom Neath 2018
All Rights Reserved

THE BET

In September 2007, our two part-time members of staff had left the company to attend their respected college courses, leaving Mr.G to recruit two new employees to fill the voids - and that is exactly what he did.

The two new recruits had just finished sixth form and were debutants in the world of work, so a considerable amount of training was required.

The new employees start dates had coincided with Mr.G's annual leave, so it was agreed that I would train one new employee and Mr.S would train the other new employee. To add a little spice to the proceedings, myself and Mr.S had a little bet. The bet was simple - the new employee which had taken the most amount of money by the end of their first day would win the bet for their trainer. The winnings consisted of a crate of larger, so there was plenty at stake here!!!

GAME ON! A coin was tossed to decide which new employee myself and Mr.S would be teamed up with, and boy was lady luck not on my side! IN THE BLUE CORNER! Mr.S's young protégé - an eighteen year old female that was smartly presented, intelligent and had a desire to learn the ropes. IN THE RED CORNER! I had the opposite! A scruffy eighteen year old male that looked like he would much rather be at home playing on his gaming console. If I was to win this bout, it would eclipse anything that Rocky Balboa had achieved, that is for sure!

I decided to gently bed in my new employee by asking him about his hobbies and interests - computer games and cars was his mumbled response.

Trying some sarcastic humour this time, I asked,

"So, why do you want to work in a camping and outdoor shop? Is it your love of the great outdoors?"

My new employee's second mumbled response came in these words.

"Because my mum told me to get off my backside and get a job."

The enthusiasm to train up my new employee was going in the same direction as the prize crate of lagers - slowly over the horizon! Never the less, there was pride at stake so I was not prepared to throw the towel in just yet.

I neglected to go straight into product training with my new employee, as I did not regard him to be at the level where he could or would want to take in the knowledge. Instead I decided to concentrate on some basics in customer service. As I started,

Copyright © Tom Neath 2018
All Rights Reserved

my new employee pulled his mobile phone out of his pocket and started texting! Cheeky sod! I told him, in no uncertain terms, that he was not allowed to have his mobile phone on the shop floor and that staff's personal belongings are to be kept in the staff room. He then moaned that he was hungry and asked if he could go out and get a burger! I reminded him that he had only just started his shift! He sighed, and I took deep a breath and attempted to go over the basics in customer service.

"Now, when a customer enters the shop, what is the first thing that you do?'

"Um. um..' was the extent of his reply.

I could have offered my new employee the latest games console for answering correctly and he still would not have got the right answer! I put him out of his misery.

"The first thing that you do is greet the customer" and with that, a customer enters the shop and - hold the front page - my new employee greets the customer! GREAT! There is a light at the end of the tunnel - or so I thought.

The customer then pulls out his mobile phone and my new employee barks out,

"Oi!, You're not allowed to have your mobile phone on the shop floor!"

I immediately apologised to the customer and explained that my colleague is a new member of staff. The customer inquiries as to whether there were any job vacancies in store. I told the customer that there were no current vacancies. I then looked at my new employee, and added that we *may* have a vacancy in the very near future!!!

Midday had arrived and I had gone through as much customer service training as my patience would allow, so just before I sent my new employee on his lunch break, I offered him some advice.

"When you come back from your break, I want to see a bit of enthusiasm for the job. Do this and you will be just fine. However, if you continue with the attitude that you have been displaying so far, you may not have a job to come back to tomorrow."

Tough words I know, but I felt that the softly softly approach would not have had any positive effect what so ever. I just hoped that my words would sink in while he indulged in his fast food fix.

Meanwhile, what a contrast Mr.S was having with his new employee - not only was she going it alone in serving the customers, but she had made just shy of £150! I thought to myself that I may as well pay out on the bet right there and then!

As I was psyching myself up for the second half of a match where the result was virtually a forgone conclusion, my employee retuned from his lunch break and I

Copyright © Tom Neath 2018
All Rights Reserved

noticed something different about him - he had a little bit of steely determination to succeed! Before I could inquire about the sudden change in attitude, a customer entered the shop and inquired about wellington boots. As there was little technical knowledge to pass on with wellington boots, I asked my new employee if he felt confident enough to serve the customer - and he said he would give it a go! Good man! I watched him bring out two pairs of wellington boots - one pair being the customer's correct size and the other pair being the next size up. A very good piece of thinking, as a lot of customers tend to wear thick socks with wellington boots and therefore go up a size. The customer purchased a pair of wellington boots and he competently processed the customer's transaction, explained our refund and exchange policy and thanked the customer for his custom. An excellent first sale for my new employee!

Had the odds of Mr.S winning the bet just been severely slashed?! Was the greatest comeback of all time now on the cards?! Mr.S's new employee was continuing to get sales through the till, so I knew that I had to come up with a cunning plan to stem the flow. Knowing that she was about to take her lunch break, I dashed to the staff room and made her a hot drink, of which she gratefully accepted. A kind gesture on my part wouldn't you say? Well, it would have been a kind gesture, if I had not laced it with a laxative!!!

"OH TOM YOU ARE A NASTY PIECE OF WORK" I hear you cry!

Well this was war and I had to win the bet. It was not just the lager at stake, it was the bragging rights.

With Mr.S's new employee 'engaged' for the rest of the shift it was the perfect opportunity for my new employee to seize the advantage! I continued to shadow him as he was talking to the customers, and I would chip in with some product knowledge when required. Hats off to him, he was now getting regular sales through the till! Needless to say Mr.S was stunned with such a turnaround in proceedings! With just ten minutes of trade left, and the deficit now reduced to just five pounds, just one more sale could see me win the bet! Then, a customer enters the shop!!! Mr.S's head drops, as my new employee darts over to the customer - GO ON MY SON, WIN ME MY BET!!! Then arrived the fatal blow to my hope of pulling off the comeback of all time - the customer said that he did not require any help as he was killing time while waiting for his bus. AAAAAAAAAAAAGH!!! I looked like a football manager that had just seen his team have a last minute winning goal ruled out for

Copyright © Tom Neath 2018
All Rights Reserved

offside!

As my heart sunk, the huge grin that had deserted Mr.S for the vast majority of the afternoon, had returned. The customer then left the shop and it was time to close and also time to admit defeat. Mr.S had won the bet despite the best efforts of my new employee, and my dastardly plan. By this time, Mr.S's new employee was over the worst of her 'troubles', understandably, she did not feel comfortable in using the bus service by means of getting home. So, feeling guilty that it was my devilish action that put her in that position, I offered her the money for a taxi of which she accepted.

The following day I asked my new employee why he had had a sudden change of attitude and he replied that he cannot help his mum to pay the bills without a job. He added that the job centre does not have a games console! Although I had lost the bet, I had won in another way, as I had helped a boy mature into a man and I was there to witness this defining moment in his life. Both of the new employees were terrific additions to the shop and it was a shame to lose them when they decided to pursue other careers.

Just for the record, if Mr.S's new employee reads this story I do genuinely regret my action, and fully accept that it was not a nice thing to do. If our paths were to cross again I would gladly buy you a drink to make up for my dastardliness. If I thought for one second that you would accept a drink from myself!!!

Copyright © Tom Neath 2018
All Rights Reserved

A SHOPLIFTER WITH STANDARDS

Shoplifting. Not a particularly pleasant subject I grant you, so thankfully the incidents involving shoplifters were few and far between. Why were shoplifters only rarely enticed in to the shop I hear you ask! Well, I will tell you. As previously mentioned our stock consisted of low to middle value brands, not the high value brands - and this is what the shoplifters craved. The shoplifters knew that the top brands are what fetches the big money in the murky waters of the black market. You would never see our £9.99 ponchos being offered to the punters around the local pubs! But as the stock was not nailed to the floor there was always the risk that that one of these vile excuses for a human being would try their luck at reducing our stock levels without handing over so much as a copper coin in return. This proved to be the case on one morning in autumn 2008.

I was alone on the shop floor as Mr.S was on a day off and Mr.G had to pop out to get his wife's birthday present (I'm not sure how fond he is of her, as he asked me if I knew whether or not Poundland sell gift cards!!!)

The telephone, situated at the back of the shop, started to ring, so I broke off from my tidying at the front of the shop to answer the call. The telephone call consisted of a customer inquiring about the range of socks that we stocked. Knowing the huge range of socks that was stocked, all I can say is that I was glad that I was not paying for the telephone bill!

Fifteen minutes into the conversation, I noticed a boy in his mid-teens enter the shop wearing the shoplifter's uniform, as I called it, consisting of a baseball cap, a black puffer jacket, dirty jeans and trainers.

Now, I hate to be stereotypical, actually what the heck, I'll be stereotypical, I was as sure as I could be that he had not just joined the Ramblers Association and was looking to get kitted out, and that he was in fact in my shop with the intention to shoplift.

One of the golden rules in retail is that you never break off from a customer, whether they are in person or communicating through the telephone, unless it is a life or death situation. With this in mind, I politely tried to close the conversation with my telephone customer in order to keep a closer eye on the boy, but my customer's questions continued to come thick and fast. The boy lingered around the front of the

Copyright © Tom Neath 2018
All Rights Reserved

shop, constantly looking at the jackets and then over at myself, and I was bracing myself for him to perform a 'snatch and run' - and after a few more seconds my prediction came true! The thieving little tyke had stolen an armful of jackets!

After a further five minutes, my telephone conversation finally concluded, when the customer announced that she never purchases a product without 'seeing it in the flesh' so she would pop in to the shop later on that day.

Then one of those 'hold the front page' moments took place - if you think that both the shooting of John F Kennedy and the fall of the Berlin wall was headline news, than you ain't seen nothing yet! This thieving little tyke came back into my shop, armed with the jackets that he had just stolen!!! *"Have you returned for the matching over trousers?!"* I thought to myself. No, he had not. Instead he bellowed these words...

"I DON'T WANT THESE COATS, THEY ARE CRAP!!!"

He then throws the jackets on to the floor and darts out of the store! I could not believe what I had just witnessed - a shoplifter with so much contempt for what he had just stolen, would rather return the stock back to the shop than suffer the embarrassment of trying to sell his ill-gotten gains!!! The characters of Broadmead never cease to amaze me.

I had just finished putting the returned jackets back into their rightful place when Mr.G, unaware of the event that had just occurred, enters the shop. (Clutching a small Poundland bag!) He pointed at the jackets that I had just assembled and commented that they have been in store for a long time and that he may have to reduce their price if we are to have any chance of selling them. I thought is there any point? We can't even give them away!!!

Copyright © Tom Neath 2018
All Rights Reserved

THE AREA MANAGER

I have found the vast majority of the Area Managers that I have encountered down the years to be egotistical and hard to please (even when the shop is hitting its targets).

One Area Manager had issued a written warning to a Manager in another branch for simply having an idea regarding the positioning of stock. I kid you not folks. But, and I say this through gritted teeth, I would have swapped the Area Manager in this story with any of the pre mentioned Area Managers.

In all my time working for the camping shop there was only one incident that had occurred which warranted disciplinary action of the highest order, and this incident occurred in autumn 2005. Mr.G had just taken on a new member of staff who, and this is putting it politely, was an oddball to say the least! A couple of days into the oddball's first week with us, I had arrived for work one morning and noticed that Mr.G was looking very tired. I asked if he had got much sleep the previous night and he replied no, as he had a phone call from the police at 2am! I jokingly commented that the boys in blue had finally caught up with him then!? Mr.G glared at me. Time to stop joking Tom.

I asked Mr.G what the telephone call was about.

"The police informed me that the shop alarm had been activated and I was required to come all the way into town to deactivate the alarm. I was met by a policeman outside the shop, and as we were checking the premises, we noticed that a window in the stock room had been smashed, but strangely, nothing was taken."

By this time it was 4am, so Mr.G cleaned up the shattered glass, boarded up the window frame with cardboard and spent what little of the night there was left at the shop, tucked up in one of the sleeping bags! Well, head office do like us to test out the products!

Oddball then turns up for his shift, to which he is greeted by Mr.G, and he informs the oddball about the previous night's break in. The words that then came out of the oddball's mouth hit myself and Mr.G for six.

"Oh, I know about the break in. It was me."

After a few seconds of shocked silence, Mr.G asked the oddball to repeat the

Copyright © Tom Neath 2018
All Rights Reserved

comment.

"I broke into the shop last night" the oddball reaffirmed.

Mr.G and I looked at each other in disbelief! Realising that the oddball was telling the truth, Mr.G asked him why he had carried out this criminal act.

"Because I left my coat here" he answered.

Upon hearing the oddball's unbelievable response, I checked the date to make sure it was not April the first! The oddball continued.

"There was no one in the shop to let me in, so I had no choice but to smash the window"

Mr.G finally lost his cool and snapped.

"OF COURSE THERE WAS NO ONE IN THE SHOP- IT WAS TWO O CLOCK IN THE MORNING!!!"

Mr.G took a deep a breath and, in a calm tone, asked the oddball why he could not have waited until the next day to pick up his jacket? The oddball simply shrugged his shoulders.

Mr.G asked me to take the oddball to the staffroom while he decided on the next course of action. Now this was hardly a run of the mill situation, wouldn't you agree? With this in mind, Mr.G made a telephone call to the Area Manager seeking some guidance. The Area Manager arrived later that morning and what proceeded was even more unbelievable. The Area Manager strolled in to the store, calmly walked up to the oddball, waggled his cheek and in a joyful tone bellowed,

"YOU'RE A CHEEKY CHAPPY AREN'T YOU!"

Time for the second disbelieving look to take place between myself and Mr.G! A cheeky chappy!? A fucking cheeky chappy!? Goodness me, this oddball has just broken in to the shop and all the Area Manager could say was that he is a CHEEKY CHAPPY!!! He continued.

"Now, I'm sure that oddball is very sorry for his actions and I am sure that this will not happen again. I think that the best way forward is to forget about the incident. Oh before I forget, next week's delivery time has been changed."

Time for the third disbelieving look to take place between myself and Mr.G!

Forget about the incident?! Any other Area Manager, and any other company come to think of it, would have sacked the oddball on the spot! I asked the Area Manager who was going to pay for the window repair.

"Oh, just take it out of petty cash" he replied, like it was a just an annoying

Copyright © Tom Neath 2018
All Rights Reserved

afterthought!

After his failed attempt to change the conversation by using next week's change of delivery time, the Area Manager again attempts to change the conversation.

"Now, how is trade?"

Mr.G, visibly annoyed at how serious the incident is failing to be taken, keeps his answer short and sweet. The Area Manager then brings his visit to an end and as he made his way to the doors he notices some dust on a clothes stand, and comments.

"Make sure that you give the shop a good dusting before my next visit, otherwise I will have to start dishing out the sackings! BYE!"

The son of a bitch. I am sure that you can imagine all the other words that myself and Mr.G used to turn the air very, very blue. We did not know who we were more angry with - the oddball for his actions or the Area Manager for his lack of carrying out the *right* actions! For the record, this Area Manager held this role with company longer than any other Area Manager! The phrase 'friends in high places' comes to mind!

I think that the oddball realised that Mr.G no longer wanted him working in the shop and a couple of days after the incident the oddball handed in his notice stating that he was relocating to Knutsford. A very aptly named place indeed.

Copyright © Tom Neath 2018
All Rights Reserved

CARELESS TALK COSTS WIVES!

Mr.G took great pleasure in performing impressions and, in particular, impersonating different nationalities. Top of the list of favourite nationalities to impersonate was the Chinese. Upon a Chinese customer leaving the shop, an impression from Mr.G was guaranteed!

So, imagine Mr.G's delight, and Mr.S's despair when a group of thirty Chinese tourists enter the shop! On one afternoon in spring 2004, this was exactly what happened.

The group did not require assistance and were quite content to browse around of their own accord. Mr.G's wife was in town and popped in to the shop to drop some lunch off for her beloved husband, and they indulged in a little conversation.

I had processed the transactions, consisting of waterproof trousers, for some of the tourists who then left the shop - CUE THE IMPRESSIONS!!!

Mr.G immediately dived into character and bellowed some Chinese sounding dialogue, joined by some highly animated Kung Fu moves which he paraded around the shop! Oh joy. Now, although I found this silliness amusing when I first joined the shop, after the fiftieth re-emergence of his Chinese impression, it does tend to lose a little of its humour. Or perhaps I was starting to mature? Either way, as Mr.S and I had yet to locate the entrance to the escape tunnel, I went to the front of the shop to tidy and Mr.S went off to make his de-stressing cup of tea!

After five minutes of parading these antics around the shop, the wife of Mr.G was trying to get his attention. *"Mr.G.! Mr.G.!"*

Her calls were to no avail, as Mr.G was having far too much fun! Her third call was in a much more desperate tone. *"MR.G!!!"*

Just why was she so anxious to get Mr.G's attention? Well I will tell you. From behind a clothes stand appeared a Chinese couple, clearly oblivious to the fact that their group had left the shop, and they were in full view of Mr.G'S antics! To say the Chinese couple look unimpressed would be a huge understatement! Mr.G, with thanks to his wife, finally spots the Chinese couple and his antics came to a sudden halt!

Now, the only way the couple could exit the she shop was to walk pass Mr.G! As the song goes 'there may be trouble ahead.' The couple slowly shuffled towards

Copyright © Tom Neath 2018
All Rights Reserved

Mr.G, arrived by his side, and stared at him! If the couple could have spoken English then I think that the air would have turned very blue indeed!

At this point you could have cut the atmosphere with a knife! What was the couple's next move going to be? Some angry words directed at Mr.G? A request for the phone number of the company's complaints department? Or perhaps they would try out a few kung fu moves of their own on Mr.G?! In the end the couple mumbled some words in Chinese that did not sound too complementary and they shuffled out of the shop to re-join their group.

"YOU JUST CAN'T HELP YOURSELF CAN YOU? WHAT IF THEY COMPLAIN TO HEAD OFFICE AND YOU END UP WITH THE SACK?! HOW WOULD YOU BE ABLE TO SUPPORT YOUR FAMILY THEN, EH?" barked the angry wife of Mr.G and she was not finished yet!

"You did exactly the same thing at the London War Imperial Museum and we were asked to leave by security! If you do not start growing up you will find yourself a sad, lonely little man. AND YOU'RE SLEEPING ON THE COUCH TONIGHT!"

The wife of Mr.G then storms out of the shop! Mr.G, trying to hide his embarrassment, straightens an imaginary tie and tries to play down his wife's angry words by commenting that she did not really mean it. Oh I think she *did* mean it, Mr.G!!!

It was strangely comforting to know that it was not just at work where Mr.G likes to take on the role of the clown!

Copyright © Tom Neath 2018
All Rights Reserved

THE MYSTERY SHOPPER

The mystery shopper folks - the bane of every shop assistant's working life throughout the land. To anyone that is not familiar with a mystery shopper, they are people employed by Head Office, to go around the shops posing as a genuine customer. Their brief is simple - to test, at random, a shop assistant on their customer service, product knowledge, competent use of the till etc etc and then report back to head office with their findings.

During my whole career I have served just one mystery shopper and scored (drum roll please.) a highly respectable 87 per cent! But despite this highly respectable score, and I make no apologies for my next comment, I have no time whatsoever for these mystery shoppers due to the next couple of incidents that I am going to share with you.

I have worked with a lot of people that are just as skilled and consistent at their job as I am, BUT, have had some horrific Mystery Shopper reports (I have seen these reports in writing). I thought how can this be? Well, after Mr.S was assessed by a mystery shopper in spring 2012, I would get my answer.

Mr.S, who I rate as the person with finest level of customer service and selling skills that I have ever worked with, had been given a score of just 23 per cent - a disastrous score that would incur disciplinary action from head office.

Mr.S had strenuously denied giving such bad customer service, and before head office could get the wheels in motion for an investigation, he threatened to resign over the matter. Well, head office took one look at Mr.S's highly commendable sales figures history reports and, surprise surprise, they dropped the matter! Funny that! Well done to Mr.S for sticking to his guns.

A couple of weeks after this incident I got the little bit of proof that I craved, which backed up my theory that some of these mystery shoppers make these reports up as they go along.

Mr.G took a telephone call from head office stating that the mystery shopper that had awarded just 23 per cent to Mr.S. had in fact made the whole report up! Mr.G was also informed that mystery shoppers would no longer be deployed. Hooray! Balloons and party poppers at the ready! However, Mr.S was still very angry about the situation - and rightly so. He takes great pride in his customer service and selling

Copyright © Tom Neath 2018
All Rights Reserved

skills, so for a complete stranger to walk in off the street and write bullshit about him, is completely unacceptable.

Although the matter had been dropped by head office, he had not received a hint of an apology in any shape or form, from head office. That's pretty disgraceful on their part, wouldn't you agree?

But why the need to make up such a damning report? Well my theory, and I stress this is just a theory, is that these mystery shoppers are 'advised' by their bosses to write more negative than positive reports, then that means more visits are required in the future to see if the service has improved, and more visits of course means more payments to the companies employing the mystery shoppers. Now, I am not suggesting for one moment that all companies that employ mystery shoppers are like this, nor am I suggesting that all mystery shoppers make up their reports. But the amount of 'bad to average' reports that the shop had accumulated down the years simply did not tally with the good sales figures of the shop. Plus with a lot of verbal and written comments from customers praising our customer service, something did not add up, right?!

Now for incident number two to help back up my case that mystery shoppers are nothing but a waste of time, and in this case a hindrance.

It was winter 2007, and I was on my own on the shop floor, as Mr.G was on a day off and Mr.S was outside the shop attending to the weekly delivery. I was talking to a lady about map cases, and my goodness did she fire every question under the sun at me! It felt like I was in the 'Mastermind' hot seat!!!

During my map case sales banter, I noticed a gentleman enter the store and browse the selection of men's ski jackets, looking as though he would like some assistance. Politely and professionally, I tried gently nudging the lady towards making a decision in what map case to purchase, however the conversation lasted a further fifteen minutes! I could see the gentleman looking anxious now, so imagine my joy when the lady had finally chosen a map case to purchase! But my joy was short lived, as she then inquired about compasses!!! Goodness me lady! Anticipating another lorry load of questions, I checked the Amazon shopping website to check that they had some voice boxes in stock!!! I could see the gentleman constantly looking at his watch, I just hoped that Mr.S had finished bringing in the delivery, and that he would appear any second on to the shop floor. No chance! With Christmas just around the corner the delivery was huge!

Copyright © Tom Neath 2018
All Rights Reserved

After ten minutes, the lady chose a compass to partner her map case and the grand total for this sale came to (buckle up and hold on to your hats folks!) £7.98!!! As the lady was putting her purchases in her handbag, I noticed that the gentleman was about to leave the shop! NOOOOOOOOOOOOO! I thanked the lady for her custom and dashed over to the gentleman, apologised for the wait and asked how I could be of assistance. The gentleman replied that he wanted to kit himself and his family out with ski-wear, but did not have the time now as he had to get back to the office. DAMN! With what the customer required, he could easily have spent £300, at least! I repeat, DAMN!!!

To make matters worse, the following day I noticed the gentleman walking past the shop carrying three full bags of goods - from a rival company! For a third time - DAMN!!!

The ending of this story, however, is a good one. The lady that I was serving, where her purchase came to the dizzy sum of £7.98, was in fact my mystery shopper! Hooray!

Copyright © Tom Neath 2018
All Rights Reserved

THE TRAINING SESSION

By early 2010, the winds of recession were blowing into the shop at quite a force, and it was harder than ever to get the sales through the till, and therefore sale targets were not being met. Customer footfall was also decreasing, which of course made it even more difficult to achieve sales. In an effort to address the situation, Head Office informed Mr.G that the company's customer service training representative was due to make a special visit to the shop to help us all brush up on our customer service skills and explore new ways of enticing customers back in to the store.

I have taken the best bits from the training session and moulded them into script form. So sit back and laugh out loud to the moments which nearly gave the customer service representative a nervous breakdown.

Early morning, prior to the shop being open for trade. Myself, Mr.G, Mr.S and part-time sales assistant Ms.L are seated in a semi-circle. Mr.T, the customer service representative enters the shop floor, drinking from a coffee cup. He puts the cup on the cash desk.

Mr.S: Good morning Mr.T, how are you?

Mr.T: I'm very well thank you.

Mr.S: (*Under breath*) Give it time.

Mr.T: Good morning everyone, thank you for coming in early. Now...

Mr.G: Before we start Mr.T, as I have all my staff here, do you mind if I just bring up an issue that needs to be addressed urgently?

Mr.T: No, not at all.

Mr.G: TEA AND BUISCUIT MONEY! Mr.S I have noticed that you are twenty pence short this week, can you pay up now?

Mr.S: Yes of course (*sarcastic*) I would hate to have a visit from the bailiffs over twenty pence! I'm glad that you have got your priorities in the right order for today's training session!

(*Mr.S hands Mr.G some lose change, which he counts out*)

Mr.S: Please continue Mr.T.

Copyright © Tom Neath 2018
All Rights Reserved

Mr.T: Thank you. Now...

Mr.G: YOU'RE STILL FIVE PENCE SHORT MR.S!!!

Mr.S: For goodness sake! (*Mr.S hands Mr.G five pence*)

Mr.G: Thank you kindly. Now Ms.L, you owe...

Mr.S: CAN WE CONCENTRATE ON THE MATTER OF SAVING OUR JOBS PLEASE!!!

Mr.T: Mr.S is right, I'm sure that this matter can be sorted out another time. We only have an hour, so let's get cracking. Now the reason I am here is to go over some of the basics in customer service and to look at new ways in which we can attract customers back in to the shop. So, thinking hats on!

(*Mr.G goes to the funky winter hats, puts one on and sits back down, everyone stares at him.*)

Mr.S: What are you doing?!

Mr.G: *Thinking hats on!* Plus there is no harm in a bit of product testing.

Mr.S: Oh yeah? Do some sanity testing to!

Myself: Can I wear one too?

Mr.S: FOR GOODNESS SAKE!

Mr.T: Look guy's, we really need to get cracking with the training now (*takes a deep breath*). Why is giving great customer service so important?

Mr.G: Don't you know the answer?! You're supposed to be the company's customer service representative!!!

Mr.T: I know the answer! I want to hear it from *your* mouths!

Mr.S: Great customer service is essential, as it puts money in to the till, keeps us in a job and keeps a roof over our heads

Mr.G: Plus it keeps us in erotic literature!!!

Mr.S: Less of the "*us*" please.

Mr.T: You are absolutely right...

Mr.G: You see!

Mr.T: I meant that Mr.S is right!

Mr.G: Oh.

Mr.T: Great customer service is a must, especially as there is so much competition out there. Even Tesco are doing camping accessories these days!

Myself: The only thing they don't do are weddings!

Ms.L: Imagine if they did, your special day - Tesco's value style!

Copyright © Tom Neath 2018
All Rights Reserved

Myself: The wedding outfits would be blue and white pinstripe!

Ms.L: Walking down the aisle...the *bread* aisle!

(*Mr.G goes to the till and picks up the bar code scanner*)

Mr.G: I now scan you both...

(*Mr.G scans in item of stock - BEEP*)

Mr.G: Husband and wife!

Myself: Don't forget, the more times that you get married, the more club points you get!

Mr.T: Ha-ha, very good! Seriously guys, giving great customer service is also important, because it is a fact that when a customer leaves a shop happy, they will tell five other people about their experience, which will hopefully bring in further custom.

Mr.S: The way trade is, I think that they must have told their hard of hearing friends!

Mr.T: (*Claps hands*) BANG! The customer is in your shop. What is the first thing that we do?

Myself: Have a celebration?!

Mr.T: No. We start off with a greeting, example please?

(*Mr.G cunningly strokes an imaginary moustache*)

Mr.G: Ooh hellooooo!

Mr.T: A cheery good morning will suffice

Mr.G: What if it's the afternoon?

Mr.T: (*Sighs*) After a little browsing time, you approach the customer. What is a good question to open a conversation?

Ms.L: Would you like a half price tortoise?

Mr.T: I beg your pardon?! Why a half price tortoise?

Ms.L: Because they are easier to sell than a full price tortoise!

Mr.G: Absolutely!

Mr.S: Don't look too alarmed Mr.T, Ms.L also works in her parent's pet shop.

Mr.T: Ah, understood. Right...

Mr.G: Do you have snakes going cheap?

Myself: Snakes hiss, its birds that go cheap!

Mr.T: LOOK GUYS! Can we just concentrate on *this shop* please?! Right, approaching the customer *in this shop,* if the customer is trying on a garment a good question to open a up a conversation would be to ask if the customer has the right

Copyright © Tom Neath 2018
All Rights Reserved

size, or point out that there are other colours available.

Mr.G: What if there are no other colours available?!

Mr.T: (*Sighs.*) Or if you have a serious lack of imagination, then simply ask the customer how you can be of assistance. Once you have opened up a conversation with the customer, the next step is to build a rapport by finding out what activity they are participating in and matching it to the correct product. Other times the customer will be a lot more forward and say, for example, *"I am going to Egypt, what do I need?"*

Mr.G: Flight tickets and a passport would be a good start!

Mr.T: (*Sighs*) Ok, I'll rephrase- what would you recommend for travelling around Egypt?

Mr.G: A camel!!!

(*Mr.T looks to the heavens for help!*)

Mr.S: Sandals, lightweight shorts, wickable t shirts, wide brim hat and insect repellent are your essential items.

(*Mr.G stands and whacks away an imaginary mosquito and wags his finger!*)

Mr.G: You won't be biting me you little swine!

(*Everyone stares at Mr.G. Mr.G sits back down*)

Mr.T: Ok, Egypt was just an example. What are customers currently requesting?

Mr.G: When customers come in to the store they say (*Arnold Schwarzenegger voice*) I WANT YOUR HATS, YOUR GLOVES AND YOUR WALKING BOOTS!

(*Mr.T looks to the heavens for help!*)

Mr.T: The point is sell to the current climate. It's cold at the moment, so really push fleece jackets, thermal underwear, hats, gloves and scarves! Be enthusiastic and point out that we have some of the lowest prices in town. If we can't sell our warm wear in these conditions, then we really are in trouble!

Mr.G: (*Arnold Schwarzenegger voice*) TROUBLE? GET TO THE CHOPPER!

Mr.S: Well, this is proving to be a productive exercise.

Myself: Still, if you can't beat them, join them! I heard that Arnold Schwarzenegger has got a job hiring out books - he is now known as Conan the librarian!

Mr.G: (*Arnold Schwarzenegger voice*) I'll BE BOOK!

Mr.T: Let's swing this back to saving the company please guys.

(*Mr.G stands*)

Mr.T: That's not the indication for a superman impression Mr.G!

Copyright © Tom Neath 2018
All Rights Reserved

(Disappointed, Mr.G sits)

Mr.T: So once the customer is looking at the first price lines, what do you do to try and encourage the customer to spend a little more money?

Mr.G: (Mr Bumble, from 'Oliver' voice) MORE? MORE?!

(Mr.T picks up a first price jacket and a higher price jacket)

Mr.T: To encourage the customer to spend a little more, you simply point out the added features that you get with the higher priced garment. So for example, the differences between these two garments?

Myself: The first priced jacket is lightweight, so it's ideal for spring and summer use and will keep out a shower. With the other garment, it has a higher rating of waterproofing, has a structured hood and two security pockets.

Mr.G: (Sings, in the voice of Fagin from 'Oliver') You got to pick a pocket or two!

Mr.T: Well done.

Mr.G: (Straightens an imaginary) Well thank you Mr.T, I should be on stage!

Mr.T: (Losing cool) THE WELL DONE WAS MEANT FOR TOM!!!

Mr.S: (Points at Mr.G) Goodness me. If your name ever went up in lights, I'd pray for a power cut!!!

Mr.T: Ok, so you have shown the customer a selection of items that matches their requirements, now let's look at obstacles that could prevent us from gaining a sale.

Mr.G: Obstacles, Krypton factor (winks at Mr.T) I'm liking the game show vibe!

Mr.T: (Stares at Mr.G, deadpan) If this was a gameshow, then I am looking at the booby prize! Obstacles that can stop us gaining sales - any suggestions?

Mr.S: Dislike of colour.

Mr.G: (Bruce Forsythe voice) Ok, we are going to change the blue coat for a green coat!

(Mr.T throws arms in the air and has a look of anger)

Mr.S: Thank you very much Bruce Forsythe!

Myself: Carry on like this Mr.G and it could be a case of 'Play Your P.45 Cards Right'!!!

Mr.T: (Takes a deep breath) That's right Mr.S, if the customer is not keen on the colour, then go and have a look on the till to see what other colour options are available

Mr.G: (Bruce Forsythe voice) Don't touch the pack, I'll be right back!

(Mr.T glares at Mr.G)

Copyright © Tom Neath 2018
All Rights Reserved

Mr.T: Another obstacle is that we could be out of stock of the required size, if so, what MUST be asked?

Mr.G: (Bruce Forsythe voice) We asked one hundred customer service representatives, at any time in your career have you considered anger management therapy?

Mr.T: (ENRAGED!!!) I DON'T NEED ANGER MANAGEMENT THEROPY!!!

(Everyone stares at Mr.T, as he tries to regain his composure)

Myself: (To Mr.S) To be fair, before eight o clock this morning, he probably didn't need anger management training!

Mr.S: If we do not have the customer's correct size in stock, then we ask them if they would like the size ordered in to store.

Mr.T: That's right.

Mr.G: BRING ON THE SPEEDEBOAT!

(Everyone glares at Mr.G.)

Mr.S: Mr.G you are the answer to the question that people did not want to ask! I'm sure that murder would be legalised if the court of law knew of you!

Mr.T: Murder and game shows?! It's just your average training session really! Ok, moving on...

Mr.G: MICHAEL BARRYMORE!

Mr.T: WHAT?!

Mr.G: Michael Barrymore - he's a murdering game show host! A body was found in his swimming pool.

Mr.S: (*Stern*) Excuse me, I think you will find that his case was ruled accidental death actually, so Michael Barrymore is NOT a murdering game show host.

Mr.G: I wonder where in the swimming pool the body was found. Was it at THE TOP, THE MIDDLE, OR THE BOTTOM?!

Mr.T: (*Desperate*) Guys please can I continue with what I'm paid to do? Now, where was I?!

Myself: Seconds away from insanity!?

Mr.T: Ok, we have looked at a couple of obstacles that could prevent us from gaining a sale. Now, what can we do if the customer has their heart set on a product, but it is a little above their price range?

Mr.G: Tell the customer to go on eBay?

Mr.T: (*ENRAGED!!!*) NO! YOU ARE TRYING TO MAKE MONEY FOR THIS

Copyright © Tom Neath 2018
All Rights Reserved

COMPANY! (*Takes a deep breath*).

Myself: If the price is more than the customer is willing to pay, then we ask the customer if they are members of any groups, such as The Ramblers Association, student, forces etc.

Mr.T: That's right, we offer discount for lots of groups, so make sure the customer is aware, as this can make the difference between gaining and losing a sale. When *we are* getting the sales, don't forget to offer the add on sales, such as proofing and cleaning products

Mr.G: It's a bit difficult to get add on sales when we are barely getting *ANY SALES!!!*

Mr.S: Although a negative, that is the most sensible thing that you have said all morning!

Mr.T: Guys I understand that it is hard at the moment, but as long as we can say that we have tried. The bottom line is that we simply have to sell sell sell, sell sell sell, sell sell sell! What must we do?

ALL: SELL SELL SELL!!!

Mr.T: Excellent. Right now guys, to the second part of the training session. With customer footfall taking a severe dip, we need to find ways of attracting customers in to the store. Now, like you guys, I need my job, so I'm sure that I don't need to explain the consequences of declining custom! So, any ideas guys?

Mr.G: I know! How about I lay in wait at the front of the shop for Mr.S to push a customer in to the shop and I will hit the customer over the head, tie him up and keep him hostage until he makes a purchase.

Mr.T: Good but illegal. Next?

Mr.G: I know!

Mr.T: Is this a genuine suggestion this time?

Mr.G: Yes, in fact this idea is flawless.

Mr.T: (With dread) Ok go on then, share this flawless idea with us.

Mr.G: How about we have product demonstrations in the window?

Mr.T: (Excited) Ah, like having a staff member attaching a rucksack on to a mannequin to show how it should be fitted correctly? I like it!

Mr.G: No, I was thinking of having a one of our travel showers in the top corner of window, and let customers come in to try it out. Preferably women!

(Mr.T's head drops.)

Mr.T: So, you want naked women prancing around in the shop window getting

Copyright © Tom Neath 2018
All Rights Reserved

soaking wet in attempt to attract people in to the store?!

Mr.G: Well, it works in Amsterdam!!!

Mr.T: Great that's that sorted then! I'll get that cleared with head office, in fact head office could send their cleaner, old Doris, to come down to the shop and do a once weekly stint in the window!!!

Mr.G: Fantastic! I'll get the camera charged!

(Mr.T despairingly puts his head in to his hands)

Ms.L: You really are a perverted man, aren't you?!

Mr.G: If customers are failing to be attracted in to try the travel shower, then I may have to ask Ms.L to give it a go!!!

Ms.L: I can give you the answer to that right now, have you got the swear box handy?!

Mr.S: Ignore him Ms.L, he is just trying to wind you up. Mr.G needs some serious help.

Mr.T: I don't think that he is the only one that needs help.

(Mr.T lifts head out of hands and takes a deep breath)

Mr.T: Anyone else with some genuine ideas?

Mr.G: What?! Do you mean the travel shower idea was no good?

Mr.S: For goodness sake! You would have all the tramps coming in to the shop just to take a shower!

Mr.G: Good point, we could charge them, a new market identified!

Myself: Yes, that lucrative market of the homeless!!!

Mr.G: Ok, we won't insist on payment then, we would be doing our bit to help the homeless.

Mr.T: (*ENRAGED*) YOU WILL NOT BE HAVING A TRAVEL SHOWER IN THE WINDOW!!! YOU ARE SUPPOSED TO BE THE MANAGER OF THIS SHOP, YET YOU HAVE OFFERED NO PRODUCTIVE INPUT WHATSOEVER! IN FACT YOU HAVE BEEN AN UTTER HINDERANCE THROUGHOUT!!!

(*Mr.T takes a deep breath*)

Mr.T: This has been a complete waste of time.

(*Mr.T puts coat on and picks up laptop bag*)

Mr.T: I am going back to head office now...

Mr.G: To ask about the travel shower?!

Mr.T: NO! I report back to head office after every training session, and believe me,

Copyright © Tom Neath 2018
All Rights Reserved

nothing will be left out from this sessions findings!

(*Mr.S looks at watch*)

Mr.S: But the training session was not an hour long!

Mr.T: Well for once I don't mind finishing early!

Mr.S: Funny that.

(*Mr.G shows Mr.T to the door*)

Mr.G: Well thanks for coming in this morning. Same time, same place, next year?

Mr.T: Certainly, just without me!!!

(*Mr.T exits the shop. Mr.G takes off his wacky winter hat and returns it back to its rightful place*)

Mr.S: (*To Mr.G*) Are you not worried about what Mr.T will say to head office?

Mr.G: Nah, I have attended his training sessions before, while being just as entertaining, and there have never been any repercussions!

Myself: Well I hope that you're right. After seeing how stressed he was, he is doing one of three things - (1) going to head office as stated, (2) find the nearest open pub or (3) he is going to call the Samaritans!!!

End of scene.

So this training session folks, I think that you would agree, is one of the funniest that you have been present at, right? Mr.G must have had someone from the heavens looking down on him as head office never brought up his training session antics. The following week, in an effort to attract customers in to the shop an emergency 25 per cent off sale was introduced, and it had the desired effect. So for a while at least, trade was on the up and all was rosy again.

Copyright © Tom Neath 2018
All Rights Reserved

CELEBRITY SHOPPERS

Celebrities visiting my shop was nearly as rare as rocking horse droppings! On the very few occasions that I have served a celebrity, I ended up learning a couple of valuable lessons. One of the lessons being that not all celebrities have as much financial clout as you may think!

My first experience involving a celebrity came in 2007. The celebrity on this occasion is an actor that has appeared in television programmes, including the medical drama 'Holby City' and long running soap opera 'Coronation Street'. As this actor entered the store, I cheerfully greeted him and he mumbled back *"alright?"* without making eye contact. Charming! He was in earshot of myself greeting other customers that entered the shop, so he would have known that I had not singled him out because of his celebrity status. He browsed around and after a couple of minutes I asked him if he would like some assistance.

"Nah, I'm just having a look" was his sulky reply.

I started hanging some stock from delivery, and the celebrity took a phone call that certainly did not improve his mood! After a minute of him sighing, and puffing of the cheeks, he hung up and mumbled the words,

"Bloody re-shoots" and stomped out of the shop. Celebrity's certainly have bad days too folks!

Another celebrity experience came about a year later, and this time the experience was a lot more pleasurable. If I said that this celebrity always had 'a cunning plan' you may very well know who I am referring to! After a pleasant exchange of greetings, the celebrity inquired about waterproof over trousers. I entwined my sales dialogue with a little social banter, as I told him that I am a fan of his work, and he was very humble at my appreciation. He politely inquired about my hobbies and I replied that I like to write comedy and he generously gave me a few tips on how to go about getting my work looked at. He then selected a pair of waterproof trousers to purchase and, as I processed his payment, he thanked me for my excellent service and wished me luck with my writing projects. This celebrity was an absolute gentleman and a pleasure to serve.

My final celebrity experience came in early 2011, courtesy of serving a well-known female pop star. A lady entered the shop wearing a flat cap, sunglasses and

Copyright © Tom Neath 2018
All Rights Reserved

stylish black leather jacket and browsed around at the front of the store. I approached the lady, greeted her and, as she removed her flat cap and sunglasses, I had to blink twice as I realised who she was! Now make no mistake, this lady was certainly on the Grade A list of celebrities. I asked her if there was anything that I could help with and she replied that shortly she would be touring around some very cold climates and needed a warm jacket, fleece jackets and thermal underwear. At first I thought 'is this a wind up?!'

"Don't you celebrities have people to do this sort of thing for you?" I asked politely.

"Oh we do, but I've recently let my personal assistant go." she replied.

I showed the lady a selection of garments that matched her requests, and although not as sociable as the previously mentioned celebrity, she was polite and courteous throughout my sales patter. After half an hour, she picked out a selection of garments which came to the total of £229.83! Lovely! I asked the lady how she would like to pay and she replied 'by card please' and she nervously slotted her card in to the machine. Just as I was thinking that I could not wait to tell Mr.G who I have just served and that I have made over £200, the words came up on the card machine that every shop assistant dreads - CARD DECLINED! Aaaaaagh! I politely explained to the lady what had just happened and despite being apologetic she did not seem all that surprised that her card had declined. She requested that the goods to be held for a couple of hours and someone on her behalf would come in and collect the goods. I said that that would be fine and the lady put her sunglasses and flat cap back on and left the store. Now when we reserve items for customers, we are supposed to put the customer's name with the item(s) - how serious do you think I would have been taken by Mr.G and Mr.S if I had carried out this standard procedure?! They would have thought I had gone insane! I simply wrote 'Ms' and added her surname. Unfortunately no one came back to pick up the goods and a week later I read in a national newspaper that this celebrity had just been declared bankrupt.

Oh, the other lesson that I learnt after serving a moody celebrity, a charming celebrity and a celebrity that had their card declined, was that these celebrities are no different from the everyday customers that walk through my shop doors.

Copyright © Tom Neath 2018
All Rights Reserved

DANGER, MOUSE!

Early one morning in winter 2008, prior to being open for trade, myself, Mr.G, Mr.S and part-time sales assistant Mr.R had arrived early to sort through a huge delivery that arrived at the end of the previous day.

Mr.G had built up an appetite and announced that he was off to the bakery and asked if any of us would like anything to eat.

"A MOUSE!" Mr.R exclaimed!

Wouldn't you prefer a pasty asked Mr.G!

"LOOK! A MOUSE!" Mr.R continued.

We all looked towards where Mr.R was pointing and low and behold a mouse is exactly what we saw!

"He shouldn't be in here" cries out Mr.G *"we're not open yet!"*

We darted towards the mouse in the hope of making a swift capture, but like lighting the mouse vanished out of sight. After a further ten minutes of hunting our unwelcome guest, with no success Mr.G bellowed out that the mouse had gone to rival store to compare prices! The mouse had found the perfect hiding place and we now faced the tricky task of hunting down the mouse before opening for trade.

"Just how on earth are we going to catch the mouse?" I asked.

"I know! Let's hold a cheese party" quips Mr.G!

Mr.S asked us to start taking the situation seriously, because as well as the professional issues, we sell food products and if the health and safety department get wind of this they could close us down. Not good! This comment made us all realise how serious the situation was and, just as fast as the mouse disappeared, Mr.G was just as quick in going to the telephone stating that he's going to phone Rentokil. This sparked an outburst from Mr.S.

"Oh what a great idea, having a Rentokil van outside the shop will not arouse any suspicions will it?!"

Mr.G asked Mr.S if he had any better ideas, to which of course he hadn't. Mr.G proceeded with his telephone call, but was informed by Rentokil that there were currently no representatives available to visit the store! However, a representative should be with us by the end of the day. Oh great! No representatives?! Is the pied piper in town?!

Copyright © Tom Neath 2018
All Rights Reserved

Reeling from this crushing blow, we had a quick brain storm to come up with some ideas for catching the mouse.

"What about a shop cat?!" I jokingly suggested.

"A SHOP CAT?! How on earth are we going to explain a shop cat to the customers? asked Mr.S, who was not getting my humour in any shape or form whatsoever.

I decided to prolong the joke and replied that we tell the customers that the cat is hunting the mouse!!! As Mr.S looks to the heavens for help, Mr.G chips into the conversation, and in a disbelieving tone bellows out...

"A SHOP CAT?!" Mr.S replied that he was glad that he and Mr.G were, for once, in agreement. Or so he thought.

"A shop cat is a marvellous idea" exclaimed Mr.G!!!

"WE WILL NOT BE HAVING A SHOP CAT!' bellowed Mr.S *"It would cause unwanted attention."*

Mr.G continued his argument in support of having a shop cat.

"We will help the cat to blend in by giving it a staff uniform!"

"I think that we are just out of cat shape shirts" was Mr.S's response in an attempt to put the idea to bed."

But Mr.G was just waking this idea up as he continued.

"He will also have to have a staff name badge"

Mr.S bellowed back.

"I think that we are also out of Tabby and Ginger name badges too!"

"What if the shop doesn't catch the mouse?" I asked.

"He gets his cards" replies Mr.G!

Que another outburst from Mr.S.

"What sort of cards? The 'sorry to hear that you didn't catch the mouse' sort of cards?!"

"Now you are just being silly Mr.S" replies Mr G to an exasperated Mr.S. *"You know that cats can't read!!!"*

At this point Mr.S went off to, yes, you have guessed it, to make his distressing cup of tea!

Mr.G then gave myself a handful of change and asked me to pop down to the convenience store and pick up a couple of different types of cheese.

"Why?" I asked.

Copyright © Tom Neath 2018
All Rights Reserved

Mr.G replied that he fancied a welsh rarebit!

In a more serious tone he then said *"I want to put a selection of cheese on the cash desk, telling customers that we are supporting a local farm by promoting its cheese. But secretly, it will entice the mouse in to capture!"*

"So you are not seriously thinking about the idea of having a shop cat then?" I asked Mr.G.

"Absolutely not" he replied, *"that was all for Mr.S's benefit!!! Poor Mr.S, he falls for it every time"*.

Despite myself and Mr.R staring at Mr.G in disbelief at this idea, we both knew that he was being absolutely serious. I made my way out of the store and Mr.G barks out.

"IF THEY ARE OUT OF CHEESE, THEN BRING BACK A CAT!!!"

Midday had arrived and with the 'local farm's cheese' failing to have the desired effect (not that this came as a surprise to the sane members among us!) and with no sign of Rentokil, a new plan of action was required. Step forward Mr.G with another plan!!!

Mr.G decided that he needed a cunning disguise and, in his own words, *"so the mouse would not recognise me!!!"* I kid you not folks, these were his exact words.

So from shop stock, Mr.G put on a mosquito head net, a wide brim camouflage hat and armed himself with a fishing net! I was in two minds as to whether or not to make a telephone call to Broadmoor to let them know that one of their patients has escaped! Myself, Mr.S and Mr.R carried on with our shop duties and left Mr.G to hunt the mouse. To say that Mr.G gained some inquisitive looks from the customers was an understatement!

Four o clock came and Mr.R's shift had finished, Mr.G was still in pursuit of the mouse, Mr.S was tiding the stock and I was assisting a customer with our glove selection. I considered my customer to be homeless, as he was of a very rough appearance and had tattoos on his neck and scars across his face and he was possibly under the influence on illegal substances.

His slurred speech consisted of mainly swear words, so I asked him to tone down his language, and taking a dislike to my warning, he swore again. I told him in no uncertain terms that he would be leaving the store if continued with his colourful language. This was one classy guy folks!

Then on the opposite side of the shop I saw it. THE MOUSE!!! I discreetly tried

Copyright © Tom Neath 2018
All Rights Reserved

to get the others attention, but it was to no avail. As there were customers in the shop I could hardly shout out *"hey, there's the mouse"* now could I?!

My dilemma now was that I knew that if I turned my back on my 'charming customer' for just one second, I knew that he would be out of the door with a free pair of gloves. I weighed up which would be better for the store - the loss of a pair of gloves or the possibility of a huge fine and/or the closure of the store. Well, there was no contest folks! I dived across the shop in attempt to grab the mouse, and just as earlier, the mouse had evaded capture and very quickly disappeared - just like the 'charming customer' that I was serving. Oh, and guess what had completed the trio of disappearances? That's right, one pair of gloves.

With just half an hour of trade remaining, the Rentokil representative finally arrived much to our relief, not just so the mouse could finally be caught but so Mr.G could finally come out of his outfit! Traps were laid throughout the shop and upon entering the shop on the following morning, laying on a trap, was one deceased mouse. Mission accomplished! It was just a shame that there was only the one vile rodent that had been caught.

Copyright © Tom Neath 2018
All Rights Reserved

CHRISTMAS GREETINGS FROM MR.G

Christmas time folks - my favourite time of the year. I love everything associated with the festive period - exchanging of presents, Christmas lunch, enjoying the Morecombe and Wise Christmas special for the umpteenth time, and most importantly spending some quality time with the family. (Yes, even in the demanding world of retail, it is possible to have some time with the family at Christmas!)

Despite the good old chore of the dreaded Christmas shopping trip causing stress for customers and shop staff alike, I can honestly say that working at Christmas time was a pleasurable experience. It's all in the preparation folks! In the couple of weeks leading up to the big day, myself, Mr.G and Mr.S would turn up to work an hour before the shop opened for trade to make sure that every line of stock had a full size range, so maximum sales could be achieved. We also checked to see if any further lines of stock had been added to the existing festive promotions and made sure that a sale ticket was on each item that was included in the festive promotions. This really helped with the smooth running of the day, as customers were not waiting around to see if their size was in stock and customers were in and out of the store, with a purchase in double quick time. It is also worth noting that myself, Mr.G and Mr.S never insisted on payment for the extra hours that we put in, but the owner of the company did show his gratitude for our all our hard work throughout the year by presenting us with a bottle of wine each upon his festive visit to the store. Mr.G also had some presents for myself and Mr.S one Christmas Eve, but they certainly did not consist of a bottle of wine.

On the morning of Christmas Eve 2004, Mr.G had rang the shop to let Mr.S know that he was going to be late in to work due the Christmas traffic, and told him to go on opening up the shop. Mr.S did as instructed and it had been a busy first hour of trade, as we had taken over two hundred pounds! There was a brief lull in trade, and with myself and Mr.S appreciating the rest bite, Father Christmas bursts into the store holding two huge carrier bags full of gifts! I thought that he had better ask himself for a new watch for Christmas, as he was a little early! Or perhaps he was doing dress rehearsal for the night's outing, got lost on his way back to Lapland, and has popped in to store for a map and compass?! Father Christmas then boisterously bursts into song.

Copyright © Tom Neath 2018
All Rights Reserved

"JINGLE BELLS JINGLE BELLS JINGLE ALL THE WAY, OH WHAT FUN IT IS TO RIDE ON A ONE HORSE OPEN SLEIGH! MERRY CHRISTMAS.!!!"

"Hello Mr.G" replies Mr.S!

"WHAT? IT IS I, FATHER CHRISTMAS!" bellows Father Christmas.

Mr.S pointed at the bags that Father Christmas was holding and asks...

"Oh, does Santa shop in a well-known sex shop then?!"

In a quiet tone Father Christmas replies;

"Even Santa has needs! Ok, you have got me banged to rights, it's me Mr.G."

He pulled his fake beard down and I told him not to do that as there are little kids walking around outside! Mr.G then plonks the two carrier bags on the cash desk and bellows;

"There you go my lovelies - Merry Christmas!"

Mr.S and I looked at each other with a look of dread, yet with a touch of intrigue!

"GO ON, OPEN UP YOUR PRESENTS" barked out Mr.G.

So that's exactly what we did. Myself and Mr.S took one look inside the bags, looked at each other and in harmony said;

"Ah, just what I always wanted, a sack full of erotic video cassettes!!!"

There must have been about fifty video cassettes in each bag! Mr.G added;

"....and because I care about your health, there is a blister pack at the bottom of each bag!!!"

Ha ha! How thoughtful! Mr.S decided to let Mr.G know exactly where he stood on whether or not to accept the Christmas 'gifts'.

"Thanks, but no thanks Father Christmas, you will just have to put these presents back on the sleigh and take them back to Lapland" Mr.S insisted.

Mr.G then informs Mr.S that the video cassettes will only get thrown out otherwise, because he is now transferring over to DVD's, as his cupboard can hold more DVD's than the more space consuming video cassettes!!! I was more than happy to take Mr.S's 'gifts' off his hands, so I asked if he was sure that he did not want them.

"ODDLY ENOUGH, FIFTY PORN FILMS DID NOT FEATURE ON THIS YEAR'S LETTER TO FATHER CHRISTMAS!!!" was Mr.S's response.

Personally, I think he was in two minds whether or not to let me have them.

As I was still living with my parents, I had to think how I could get two bags of erotic video cassettes into my bedroom without my parents noticing. With no obvious

Copyright © Tom Neath 2018
All Rights Reserved

solution coming to mind, I just hoped and prayed that they would both be out in the kitchen preparing Christmas lunch, leaving me with a clear run upstairs so I could dive straight into my bedroom.

So to the bus journey home, and it was one that I would not forget in a hurry! As I was approaching my bus stop I pressed the bell, took a bag of erotic video cassettes in each hand and as I stood up. THE DAMN BAGS SPLIT!!! AAAAAAAGH!!! Erotic video cassettes covered the floor of the bus causing huge amusement amongst my fellow passengers! What embarrassment folks. I commented to my fellow passengers that the erotic video cassettes were in fact Christmas presents for the family, but I had not had the time to wrap them up. Oddly enough, I don't think that they believed me! The time it took for the bus to reach my stop felt like an eternity, but once the bus did arrive at my stop, boy you did not see my backside for dust! Still, at least I didn't have the embarrassment of explaining to my parents how I came to acquire one hundred erotic films! I am quite sure that my father's response would have gone something like;

"Goodness me, when I was your age all I got from Father Christmas was nuts, socks and two tangerines!!!"

Copyright © Tom Neath 2018
All Rights Reserved

AN ALTERNATIVE WAY TO KEEP DRY

From my first day working in the camping shop, the oddball customers were never too difficult to spot, for two simple reasons - what they wore and what they said. If a male customer entered the store dressed in women's clothing that had not lost a bet or was not about to attend a fancy dress party, I would approach with caution! If a customer entered the store and started telling me that he was a time traveller and would like some footwear that would enable him to take part in the battle of Hastings, then I would question whether the sandwiches were ever present at his picnic! But when a customer is suitably presented and their request(s) are of a rational nature, then there is no need to expect any eccentricity, right? Wrong. There is often a fine line between genius and madness and I will let you decide which of these categories the customer in this next story falls into.

In early 2004 we were experiencing some torrential rain, so bad that at one point I swear that I saw Noah's ark float past the shop! One morning during this time a gentleman in his late thirties - sharp suited and of smart appearance - entered the shop and approached myself. We exchanged a couple of sarcastic comments regarding the appalling weather and the gentleman inquired what waterproof hats we stocked. I showed him our range of waterproof hats and he picked out a hat he liked the look of. He inquired about the price and I replied that the hat was priced at £19.99. The gentleman asked if there was anything a little less expensive and I replied that there was, but the £19.99 hat was the only hat that we stock that is 100 per cent waterproof in all conditions. The gentleman took on my words, looked towards the shop doors and depressingly looked at the appalling wet weather conditions and decided to purchase the £19.99 hat.

"Can I pay in instalments?!" The gentleman sarcastically asked.

I scanned the hat through the till and the gentleman asked if he could have a carrier bag for the hat. I thought it was strange that the gentleman chose not to wear the hat straight away, but I neglected to question the fact and put the hat into the carrier bag. It is at this point when the conversation took an odd turn. The gentleman then asked me if the carrier bag was waterproof? I replied that the bag is made out of plastic, so yes, it is waterproof. The customer stared at the carrier bag for a few seconds. I'm not so naive not to realise what was going through the gentleman's

Copyright © Tom Neath 2018
All Rights Reserved

mind, but to witness his thoughts being put into practice did hit me for six! Lightening quick, he empties the carrier bag, pokes three holes through the bag AND PULLS THE BAG OVER HIS HEAD!!!

"FORGET THE HAT, I'll JUST TAKE THE BAG!" announced the customer and he swiftly exit's the shop to endure the appalling weather! As I picked my jaw off of the shop floor, I thought to myself that it just goes to show that the most predictable of people can sometimes turn out to be the most unpredictable!

Copyright © Tom Neath 2018
All Rights Reserved

THE AWARDS CEREMONY

The owner of the company was best described as someone that is not very sociable and has a dislike of public speaking, so what does he do? Hold an annual awards ceremony of course! As the ceremony was held in the Dorset County of head office's location, we booked a hotel for an overnight stay that, although we had to pay for, the travel to the venue and the food and beverages was paid for by the company and we also received a day's pay - happy days!

I was informed by Mr.G that the ceremony was held at an alternative location to our head office premises simply because the building was not at an adequate size to host such an event. My first experience of the awards ceremony came in 2003 and it was certainly one to remember.

Our partners were also invited to the ceremony, so my girlfriend dug out her finest shell suit for the event! I'm only joking of course, my girlfriend had bought a beautiful outfit for the event - and she looked stunning. As myself, Mr.G, Mr.S and our partners clambered into the minibus, Mr.G wasted no time in kicking off the entertainment! A couple of jokes dedicated to the female form (far too offensive to print) was followed by boisterous renditions of 'Pack Up Your Troubles' and 'The Wheels On The Bus!' I noticed that our partners looked a little unsettled with Mr.G's antics and Mr.S was starting to get agitated, as he did not have the option of scuttling off to make his distressing cup of tea! In an attempt to add some calm to the journey, I swung the conversation in the direction of the ceremony and asked Mr.G and Mr.S about the ceremony, as they had both been present at these events. What was the location like? Is it a fine dining menu? Is there entertainment after the award winners are announced?

"All your questions will be answered in good time" replied Mr.G.

I could not help feeling that Mr.G and Mr.S were keeping a piece of pivotal information from myself.

We arrived in the Dorset County of the location and, assuming that we would be stopping at one of the rather plush hotels that we were passing, I was glad that I had scrubbed up well for the occasion. We had a taken a turning down a little country road and to my concern we were in the middle of nowhere! I then realised that the ceremony was being held in a country estate! With excitement, I asked if this was

Copyright © Tom Neath 2018
All Rights Reserved

the case - and Mr.G told me to be patient. The journey continued along the country road for a further mile and the mini bus stared to slow down and came to complete halt outside a large, ran down scout hut! I asked myself if the minibus driver was about to relieve himself? No. Instead he opens up the side doors and ushers us off of the minibus! With the phrase 'what in the hell?!' running through my mind, Mr.G asked us to follow him over to the scout hut door of which he then knocked on.

Two seconds later the owner of the company opened the door and greeted us with these mumbled words;

"Welcome to the company's award ceremony!!!"

As we entered the scout hut the company owner, that was on edge it has to be said, shook our hands and he hung up our coats. Ah, he is doubling up as the cloak room assistant too! The first thing that I noticed was smartly dressed staff members from the other shops looking uneasy as they talked amongst themselves. I also noticed a little old lady shuffling about, putting plates of buffet food on an old wallpaper bench - classy! Next to the bench was an old rusty tea trolley holding budget price lager, bitter, red and white wine, unopened. In the corner of the scout hut was a mullet haired disc jockey setting up his nineteen eighties equipment. Then it dawned on me - this was just the meeting place of course! I asked Mr.G where the actual ceremony was taking place. I must have said this louder than I thought, as the whole scout hut fell silent!

"This is where the ceremony is being held" replied Mr.G!

Oh, I wondered if this was how the first Oscars ceremony started?! There was a knock on the door and the owner of the company opened the door to who I thought was going to be Jeremy Beadle wearing a long beard and holding a microphone informing us that this was one big prank! This was not to be, as the guests were staff from another shop. The next hour consisted of everyone making small talk, and I do not think that one person in the room wanted to be there! Well, would you?! Then the moment that we had all been waiting for had arrived - the opening of the food and beverages! One small plate full and one small drink each were the strict instructions! Oh great! Does anyone know the telephone number for the local kebab house?!

All the food and drink had been devoured inside fifteen minutes and with everyone hungry, as they were sober, the owner began announcing the award winners via the disc jockey's microphone! After stuttering through the category

Copyright © Tom Neath 2018
All Rights Reserved

winners, which included the store with highest turnover, the store with most improved sales, etc etc, the final category for the best customer service award had arrived. I knew that I had a good chance of winning this award, as I have a fantastic level of customer service with a lot of complementary customer feedback to verify this.

"Um, ok, and the winner is....Tom Neath!!!"

Hooray! Judging by the lukewarm applause, and the smiles through gritted teeth from my fellow nominees, as I collected my half bottle of budget priced champagne, I think that there was a whiff of jealousy in the air! I was informed by Mr.G that I had won the award specifically due to a customer that I had served a few months ago. The pre-mentioned customer needed a specific style of lightweight waterproof jacket in a range of sizes and colours totalling eighty units that would bring in just shy of £2,500 for the shop!

He needed the order in store by the end of the week, so as we did not have that quantity of jackets in stock, I rang round the other shops in attempt to get the order in on time and I succeeded! Boy, did I work my backside off, so the award was fully justified.

The company owner then mumbled that the disco was about to start! The disc jockey kicked off his set with Chic's hit song 'good times' and as the line 'good times, these are the good times' filled the room, I swear that I was not the only person to see irony!!! The next half hour consisted some of the cheesiest songs known to mankind and, as everyone was sober no one had the confidence to be the first person to kick start the dancing, even Mr.G was muted. The bottom line is that everyone in attendance looked as though they would rather be at a funeral! With this in mind, I decided to fake illness and leave the ceremony early. I arranged a pick up point with Mr.G for the following day, thanked the company owner for my half bottle of champagne, and myself and my girlfriend said our goodbyes and left the scout hut. Had I just had a very weird dream? I asked my girlfriend to pinch me. No, it had definitely not been a dream!!!

Soon as we arrived at our hotel, we made our way straight to the bar! The girlfriend and I gorged out on steak and chips and lashings of lager, boy did that take out the sting of a disappointing day! After this little bit of luxury, we went up to our hotel room and as we were led on the bed sipping the champagne, my girlfriend gave me a passionate kiss and, hinting at erotic liaisons, said;

Copyright © Tom Neath 2018
All Rights Reserved

"Come on Tom, let's do what you do best."

"I am not selling you a waterproof jacket at this time of night!!!" I replied.

Seriously though folks, despite being disappointed at just how low key my first company awards ceremony turned out to be, I am not going to be too harsh on the owner of the company, because it is his penny pinching methods that have enabled him to effectively run a business that has never been in the red and most importantly, provided myself with a steady income.

Copyright © Tom Neath 2018
All Rights Reserved

YOU MUST BE JOKING?!

For the vast majority of my time working for the shop, we had a good working relationship with head office, as they were reasonable in what they expected from shop staff and rewarded us financially when we had exceeded our monthly and annual targets. However, every once in a while head office would inform us of a change of procedure or carry out an action that would raise an eyebrow or two! That is the politest way that I could put it folks! Here are some examples.

Example 1

In Autumn 2011, all shops on the company had received an email from head office stating that if we required clothes hangers for stock, then we could no longer follow procedure of simply asking warehouse. Instead, we now had to ask the owner of the company directly and he would 'make a decision' on whether to send out clothes hangers to the requesting store. I know that on at least two occasions, other shops on the company had to submit a report justifying the need for more clothes hangers! I appreciate the fact that this change in procedure occurred during the tough financial climate and was a result of cutbacks, but should you really have to fight so hard for something that is so vital in the day to day running of a shop where clothing makes up 70 percent of its total stock?! Whatever next, asking permission to pull the flush?!

Example 2

Just a couple of weeks after we had received the email regarding the coat hangers, we received another email from head office, this time regarding carrier bags. The email was in much the same vain as the previous, in that we could no longer order carrier bags through the warehouse and we had to obtain permission from the company owner and if successful, the carrier bags would now be dispatched from head office. With the busy festive period on the horizon, I decided to do a bit of preparation and I decided that I would request an extra four packs of carrier bags. With the amount of carrier bags that we already had in the shop, an order for two packs would likely have sufficed, but as head office treat themselves to a week off work over Christmas, there would be no one to supply us with carrier bags if we had ran out. I emailed through the order, and it was confirmed that four

Copyright © Tom Neath 2018
All Rights Reserved

lots of carrier bags would arrive on the following week's delivery. No worries! Or so I thought.

The delivery had arrived and I pulled out the box that contained the carrier bags and as I looked inside the box I could not believe my eyes. Mr.G asked what the problem was and I replied that last week I ordered four packs of carrier bags and warehouse have sent in four.

"Well that's ok isn't it? That's what you asked for!" comments Mr.G.

I laid four carrier bags across the cash desk and said;

"Oh yeah, they have sent four in alright. FOUR CARRIER BAGS!!! IT'S COMING UP TO CHRISTMAS AND WAREHOUSE HAVE SENT US FOUR CARRIER BAGS!!!"

An obvious breakdown in communication there folks. Or, also remembering the coat hangers email, was it a sign that the company had entered some very tough financial waters, as even the basic shop essentials were struggling to be supplied?!

Example 3

Here is an extract from an email sent from head office in 2008.

To: Branches only

Subject: Power Cuts

Hi all,

There has been some debate as to what to do in a power cut. It appears to be happening more regularly and it's best to be prepared.

1. DO NOT CLOSE THE STORE;

2. Restrict access to customers to the front (safe part) of the store, don't let   them wander around! You can do this using rails, chairs or other means;

3. Use head torches from stock and make sure that staff go carefully. H&S is paramount;

4. Make sure you have a till drawer key available to take money;

5. Write hand written receipts in duplicate - give one copy to the customer. An appro book is perfect;

Copyright © Tom Neath 2018
All Rights Reserved

6. Use paper credit card system;

7. Be upbeat and enthusiastic with the customers - they love the war time spirit!

Kind regards;

Head office.

Now unsurprisingly, Mr.G, Mr.S and myself had a few issues with this email! For example:

1. What if we have sold out of all torches?! As they make terrific presents, we did actually sell out of torches on a couple of occasions over several festive periods!

2. In point 3 of the email it states that H&S paramount. H&S stands for health and safety and yes, it is paramount so why on earth are head office adamant that the shop staff walk around a partially lighted shop at serious risk of tripping or falling over causing injury! Still, as long as we get that sale for a fifty pence whistle, then that broken ankle would have been worth it!!!

3. Let me just repeat point 7. 'Be upbeat and enthusiastic with the customers- they love the war time spirit!' LOVE THE WARTIME SPIRIT?! Yes, you can't beat a good dose of mass destruction and death to put a spring in your step, can you?! Although most of our customers were born after the Second World War, I am pretty sure that our customers that were alive during this horrific time would not care to be reminded about the most evil act that this country has ever witnessed.

Thinking that maybe head office staff members had just returned from an afternoons drinking at the local pub, Mr.G made a telephone call to head office to get clarification that this email was correct - and indeed it was! Good god! We thought that the staff members in head office were all after a career in stand-up comedy! But unfortunately for myself Mr.G and Mr.S, the biggest joke was yet to come.

Example 4

Twelve months into my career with the company, Mr.G took a telephone call from head office informing him that the shop would be undergoing a re-fit in a few weeks' time. Although the shop was in a reasonable condition it certainly needed a fresh, modern look, so the news was most welcome. The telephone call continued and

Copyright © Tom Neath 2018
All Rights Reserved

Mr.G was informed that the shop would remain open during the re-fit.

"I BEG YOUR PARDON?!" exclaimed Mr.G!

Head office repeated that the shop would remain open during the re-fit. Mr.G tried to reason with head office that keeping the shop open for trade that was crammed full of workmen and their machinery, was simply not practicable! But it was to no avail - head office's final word was that the shop would remain open for trade during the re-fit. Goodness me, the health and safety officers would have a field day with us! The first thing that I asked Mr.G was;

"Is the owner of the company a fan of lawsuits then?!"

The bottom line is that head office are terrified of losing a sale, and so they are prepared to comprise its staff (and customers) health and safety to ensure that the sale of a £3.99 pair of socks are achieved! So to the re-fit.

The builders arrived at 7.30 am and were surprised, to say the least, that the shop was continuing to trade throughout the work. After the builders had devoured their breakfast, which consisted of pasties, bacon rolls and a gallon of tea, (and there was me expecting to see them with a bowl of muesli and peppermint tea on the go!) They covered all the stock in dust sheets - so the customers could not see the stock anyway! We decided that as soon as a customer entered the shop we would explain the situation, ask what they required, and dig out the item from under the dust sheets. Work then began and the early morning peace had been kicked in to touch by loud hammering, drilling, sanding, and boisterous requests from the builders for the young apprentice builder to go out and fetch the teas! During the day we had no fewer than twenty customers enter the shop and - unbelievably - they were happy just to browse around!!! Yes, fighting their way past the workmen and machinery, at risk of injury, all in the hope of making a purchase where they couldn't even see the stock!

As we were officially open for trade from under the strict instructions of our bosses, there was not one thing that we could do to prevent customers from doing this. By the end of the day we had taken about thirty pounds in sales and this was the trend for the rest of the week. The re-fit took five days to complete but according to the builders, the work would have been completed in a maximum of three days, no doubt held up by browsing customers that had entered the shop purely out of curiosity. How serious injury was avoided I will never ever know. But surely it would have been better for the shop to close for three days, get the refit complete and

Copyright © Tom Neath 2018
All Rights Reserved

resume normal trading, instead of having five days where, on not one of these days did we make enough money to cover the staff's wages! Still, head office know best, do they not?!

Despite the best efforts of the dust sheets, the stock had accumulated a lot of dust, so Mr.G, Mr.S and I had a mammoth task in front of us to get the stock looking presentable for sale. We informed head office of the situation and they informed us that they would get some help to us as soon as possible. Great, some extra pairs of hands would be much appreciated. Early the following day a parcel turned up from head office, we opened up the parcel and it contained dust cloths and a bottle of polish!!! Oh how we laughed.

So there you go folks, four examples of head offices 'wit' and 'wisdom'. I have heard that the members of head office have formed a comedy troupe and you can catch them at a comedy club near you!!!

Copyright © Tom Neath 2018
All Rights Reserved

CUSTOMERS SAY THE FUNNIEST THINGS!

The majority of customer queries and comments have been of a rational nature, but every now and again a customer would present myself with one of the above, which made me ask myself whether the customer had just escaped from the mental institution! Some of my responses could be described as a little brash or rude even, but honesty is the best policy, right?! So without further ado here is a selection of the very best customer queries and comments that I have received down the years.

We stocked an item called a global positioning system, so I guess this question was always bound to be asked -
Customer: Does a global positioning system work abroad?
There is a clue in the title sir.

Customer: I want this rucksack, if I cut off all the bit's that I don't want, will you make it cheaper for me?
Certainly sir, but then I would have to apply a vandalism charge, which would bring the rucksack back up to full price!

Customer: These shorts are a bit short aren't they?!
Well that's the point of shorts isn't it sir?!

Customer: My husband and I are looking to purchase a pair of walking boots but we don't need them to be fully waterproof as we only intend to walk in light rain.
Two points, one - why would you intend to walk in light rain, and two - what if the rain turns heavy, madam?!

Customer: This torch is bit bright isn't it?!
That's the point of a torch isn't it?!

Customer: Tell me young man, how much of my head will this sun hat cover?
Well, it's just a guess madam, but probably no more than the perimeter of the hat!!!

Copyright © Tom Neath 2018
All Rights Reserved

Customer: Are these shoes any good for walking?

Well there is very little else that you can do in them madam!

Customer: Do you sell waterproof coats with only one arm?

If we did, I think that someone in the buying department is going to get the sack!

Customer: Can you tell me where the nearest massage parlour is please?

No need to ask who I brought in to the conversation at that point. Mr.G, are you free?!

Customer: Do you sell portable Marmite?

Well the customer would have either loved or hated my response - what on earth is portable Marmite sir?! Does it grow legs and trot over to yourself?!

Customer: Hi, I bought this compass for my Dad but I would like to return it for a refund because although it points north and works perfectly well, it's not doing what it's supposed to.

I neglected to inquire as to exactly what her Dad expected the compass to do because sometimes you simply have to admit defeat.

Customer: I was in here a year ago looking at waterproof jackets, do you remember me?

Oh yes, of course! You're Mr.Smith of 14 Clarence Road! I sarcastically replied!

Customer: This jacket states that it is windproof so does that mean that I can fart in it and no can tell?!

That's right madam, it's the only jacket that we stock that has the new, much sought after fart free feature!

While taking a customer through my range of fleece jackets, he entwined the conversation with -

How many bricks make up his house;

How many bristles are on his toothbrush; and

How many cornflakes he had in his breakfast bowl that morning.

Copyright © Tom Neath 2018
All Rights Reserved

A customer with far too much time on his hands, and dare I say it, a social reject. I'm guessing that he looks forward to the monthly bills, as it is his only form of fan mail!

Customer: Wow! This sixty five litre rucksack is lightweight isn't it?!
That's because it is empty sir!

Customer: Will the receipt say that I purchased a pair of gloves?
No madam, it will say that you purchased the Eiffel tower!

Customer: Do you sell a head torch for a nine year old dog with bad eyesight?
I must have been barking mad, because despite suggesting that a vet would be better qualified to assist, I showed the customer our range of head torches and the customer bought one!

I was showing a customer my range of walking boots and he informed myself that he intends to climb the world's five highest mountains, except Kilimanjaro.
"Why not Kilimanjaro?" I inquired.
Customer: Because I do not want to undertake a challenge with the words Kil-I-man in its name!!!

Customer: Can I put on your best fleece jacket and go outside for a walk to see if it is warm enough?
Yes, why not! I don't know you from Adam and I have only been talking to you for twenty seconds, but I fully trust you to bring my most expensive fleece jacket back to the shop!!!

Customer: Can I pierce this gas cartridge and light it instead of buying a cooker as a means of cooking food?
Certainly sir, as long as you think that you can get by in life without the use of your hands!

Copyright © Tom Neath 2018
All Rights Reserved

A customer entered the store that was quite clearly a few sandwiches short of a picnic and approached myself at the cash desk –

Customer: Do you sell anything for cockroaches?

I waited for the customer to say that he was only joking, which did not come so I asked if a little bowler hat or a sparkling bow tie would do? This was greeted by a blank stare from the customer, so I decided to break his day by informing him that we only cater for the slightly larger market of the human being!

Customer: Oh, I will just have to go where I usually go to get my cockroach goodies then, won't I.?

WHERE IN THE HELL DOES HE USUALLY GO?!

Customer: Apart from warm wear, what do you have that is suitable for ninety year old woman that is blind and deaf?

After jokingly suggesting a full set of ski gear, I politely informed the lady that we may have come to a dead end!

A teenager came into the shop, and although his inquiry was odd, the reason behind his inquiry was pretty sane -

Customer: Do you sell roller skate wheels, as I am walking in Cornwall this weekend and if I come across the Bodmin beast, I'll attach them to my walking boots in order to make a quick get away!

Genius!

Customer: Will one of your cool bags keep a chocolate dog from melting in a car for two days on the Mendips?

Bear with me madam while I just check the chapter in my training manual entitled 'keeping chocolate dogs cool while on the Mendips!'

Upon processing a customer's payment, I noticed that the customer had a carrier bag full of wines and spirits. I commented that someone's going to have a great weekend!

Customer: Yes, me! I've just come out of rehab, so I'm celebrating!!!

Copyright © Tom Neath 2018
All Rights Reserved

Customer: Do you have a stainless steel vanity mirror suitable for a parrot?
Yes certainly sir, it is just in with parrot make up accessories!

During a very quiet afternoon, both Mr.S and I had assisted a customer, as he had a long list of items and he sounded exactly like the animated Looney Tunes character Porky Pig! Just before I started scanning his items through the till, I asked the customer if there was anything else that he was looking for?

Customer: Th-th-th-that's all folks!!!

As the customer was leaving the store he took a mobile phone call and his pleasant mood soon changed to one of anger. I thought that there was no need to get so ANIMATED!!!

So, some interesting customer queries and comments there I think that you would agree, and with the bible in hand I swear that they are all one hundred per cent genuine.

Copyright © Tom Neath 2018
All Rights Reserved

ON YOUR BIKE: PART 2

The last few chapters have seen Mr.G's winding up of Mr.S take a back seat. Well it's back with a vengeance now folks! This time, Mr.G will raise the bar a lot higher than simply attaching a 'just married' sign and empty food tins to his bike.

One morning in early 2012, Mr.S had arrived for work as normal with his bike in tow, but as the weather consisted of very heavy rain, he decided to keep his bike in the dry surroundings of the stockroom. After a quiet morning that had consisted of myself, Mr.G, Mr.S and our new starter sorting through a delivery, myself and Mr.S decided to take our lunch break at the same time. Contrast to myself usually having lunch in the staff room, I met my girlfriend for lunch and doing this meant that I was absent from an act by Mr.G that even I would go as far to say is out of order. I had returned from my lunch break to see a very angry Mr.S holding his bike directing some very angry words at Mr.G. An uneventful morning was just about to get very eventful.

I asked Mr.S what was wrong and what happened was this - the new starter had shown only mild interest in helping with the delivery, so Mr.G felt that he would be better deployed at the front of the shop, making sure that customers were being greeted. Within two minutes a man in his late twenties of rough appearance wearing dirty jogging clothing entered the store and asked the new starter if the shop sold bikes. The new starter, still getting acquainted with what the shop sold, bellows out to Mr.G as to whether the shop sells bikes. Mr.G, with his head buried in a box of delivery stock and only partially listening, bellows back;

"If you can't see what you're looking for on the shop floor, then always check the stockroom."

With that, the new starter wanders off to the stockroom and shortly returns to the shop floor. WITH MR.S'S BIKE!!! He wheels the bike past Mr.G, who still has his head in a box and approaches the man.

"Here, that's a good bike ain't he!?" exclaimed the man. *"What's the damage?"*

The new starter, not knowing that 'damage' is an alternative word for 'price', replied that *there is no damage!*

"Oh great!" bellows out the man and he then hops on the bike and rides towards the doors!!! Then just in the nick of time Mr.S enters the shop and is gobsmacked

Copyright © Tom Neath 2018
All Rights Reserved

to say the least to see his bike about to be ridden out of the shop! He blocks the man's route out of the shop and demands to know what he is doing with his bike. The man replied that it is *his* bike, as that new starter had given it to him free of charge! He then again attempts to ride out of the shop and is blocked by Mr.S. who informs the man that he is not leaving with the bike.

Mr.S informed myself that it was like scene from a western film, where two gunslingers were about to draw their guns and engage in battle, though the outcome would certainly be decided before dawn! Make no mistake, Mr.S can handle himself in the face of conflict and would easily have had this man for breakfast, but as a family with young children had just entered the shop he did not want to make a scene. Mr.S then spots a couple of dvd's in the man's pocket, whips them out and asks the man how he came to acquire them.

"I bought them!" the man snapped.

Mr.S asked to see his receipt and the man barked out that he had not been given one.

"No, you don't get a receipt for proof of theft" quipped Mr.S!

He informed the man that if he did not leave the shop, without the bike and dvd's, then he would be straight on to the security radio to inform the police about the dvd's. The man hops off of the bike, mumbled some unpleasantry words at Mr.S and leaves the shop. Minus the bike and dvd's. Very well handled Mr.S!

Now as you can imagine, a very angry Mr.S had a few questions for Mr.G! Mr.G said that he was oblivious to the situation, as he was occupied with the delivery and it was the fault of the new starter. But after hearing the new starter's account of what happened, Mr.S did not believe for one second that Mr.G was oblivious to the situation and saw it as yet another act to wind him up, but this time Mr.G had crossed the line. With the patience of Mr.S finally snapping, he wrote a very stern letter to head office and their response was to hand Mr.G a verbal warning over the situation. I have to say that I did not believe Mr.G's account either, as he was only a few feet away from the situation, and I'm sure beyond reasonable doubt that he would have known exactly what was going on. In fact, he wanted the naive new starter to sell Mr.S's bike. With the verbal warning from head office causing a 'cold war' effect between the two, was this finally the end of Mr.G's antics against Mr.S?

Copyright © Tom Neath 2018
All Rights Reserved

TAXI FOR MR.S!

In the days that proceeded, Mr.G's verbal warning from head office the atmosphere inside the shop could be cut with a knife! Mr.G deliberately stayed out of the way of Mr.S - only urgent work related issues would engage them in limited communication.

Despite the verbal warning, there was no doubt in my mind that Mr.G was in fact hatching another plan to wind up Mr.S in retaliation. It could not be proven that Mr.G was the brains behind the event that next occurred, but if Mr.G did indeed carry out an act of revenge then Mr.S and I were convinced that this was it.

It was a week after the bike incident and Mr.G was on a day off. I had just returned from my lunch break, and just as Mr.S was about to take his lunch break, a chap in his early fifties, wearing a flat cap and holding a set of car keys, enters the shop. Mr.S greeted the chap, who clocked Mr.S's name badge and he replied;

"Good afternoon Mr.S, taxi!"

Mr.S apologised to the chap and said that we are out of stock of taxies!

"No, I mean your ordered taxi is here!" the chap responded.

Mr.S then asks if the taxi is going to sanity central, if so he was in! The tone of the chap then got a lot more serious.

"Look chief, the taxi that you have ordered is outside"

Mr.S, now realising that this chap is not joking, replied that there must be some mistake. But the chap was adamant that Mr.S had ordered a taxi! The chap looked at his mobile phone and read out loud.

"Taxi for Mr.S picking up from this shop at 1pm." This time the chap had read out the full name of Mr.S.

Mr.S had a look of bewilderment, then began to lose his cool and bellows at the chap.

"Why would I order a taxi?! I am half way through my shift!"

"'Well the taxi was ordered in your name, chief!" barked the chap.

"WELL I CAN ASURE YOU CHEIF, I HAVE ONE HUNDRED PER CENT NOT ORDERD A TAXI!!!" Mr.S retorted.

Now that Mr.S was starting to get animated, I attempted to inject a little calm into the situation and suggested to Mr.S that he should go and take his lunch so he could

Copyright © Tom Neath 2018
All Rights Reserved

have his destressing cup of tea. I asked the chap if he has tried to dial back the number that the booking was made on, and the chap replied that the number was withheld. Just as Mr.S was about to exit the shop floor the chap, not yet willing to admit defeat, asks Mr.S if he was sure that he had not ordered a taxi?

"QUITE SURE!!!" barks Mr.S!

The chap finally admits defeat and leaves the shop, minus a passenger. Mr.S quickly returned to the shop floor, no calmer than when he had left. I joked with Mr.S that after all that banter he forgot to give the chap a tip!!! Mr.S glared at me and said;

"...and here's a tip for you - quit the jokes"

Ooops. Mr.S then left the shop to pick up some tea bags - what a time to run out! He had better bring back a skip's worth tea bags!

When Mr.S returned from lunch, his standard tea fix had the desired effect as calm had been restored. I commented that the incident involving the taxi driver was a little odd, to say the least.

"Wasn't it just!" replied Mr.S. *"What was even more odd was the fact that the chap knew my full name, only my first name is on my name badge!"*

Myself and Mr.S put two and two together and came up with. Mr.G!!! This was a message that Mr.G no longer wanted Mr.S's presence in the shop and had ordered a taxi to take him away! But as previously mentioned, with no proof, Mr.S let this sleeping dog lie and decided against bringing up the incident with Mr.G, who interestingly had a spring in his step when he returned from his day off. But Mr.S was about to ensure that some comeuppance was served to Mr.G in an act that would result in a change to the rest of their working relationship.

Copyright © Tom Neath 2018
All Rights Reserved

MR.S TAKES HIS REVENGE

As good a sales person as I am, Mr.S was the jewel in the crown. As previously mentioned Mr.S had an exceptional sales record, and on only rare occasions would he not be top of the sales figures, not just for the shop, but for the South West area.

One week after the taxi incident, Mr.G was about to get a taste of what life would be like without the selling skills of Mr.S.

On the first day of my two week break abroad, Mr.S had taken an urgent telephone call from his girlfriend informing him that one of his close family members had been taken seriously ill, and with the permission of Mr.G, immediately left the shop and travelled up north to the location of his ill relative and remained there for two weeks. Mr.G was left with just one member of staff - the new starter mentioned in the two previous chapters! I received a call from Mr.G asking, *begging* in fact, if I could come back from my holiday to cover Mr.S's absence!

"I BEG YOUR PARDON?!" was my first response, I then sarcastically said *"Oh sure, just let me finish my pina colada and I'll be right with you!!!"*

I expressed my sympathy to his situation, but told him that leaving my girlfriend on her own, in sun drenched Tenerife, was simply not going to happen! A perfectly reasonable response, right?! But something that was not reasonable was the reaction from head office, as their first action was to give Mr.G a severe telling off for letting Mr.S go to visit his ill family member with myself already on holiday. A little harsh wouldn't you say? Mr.G could hardly say to Mr.S that he couldn't go to visit his ill family member now could he?!

Mr.G was then instructed to ring around the nearest stores to arrange cover. Now with staff cutbacks in full force, the other shops were hardly heavy handed in the staff numbers department! On the days when Mr.G could arrange cover for the shop, it was always the 'wally' that was sent from the other store (to be fair, the sending shop would hardly send out their top members of staff now, would they?!) Basically, for two weeks, Mr.G was in the brown messy stuff right up to his neck!

Three days into the absence of myself and Mr.S, the shop drastically failed to hit the daily target and the telephone calls from head office soon started to engulf the store.

"WHY HAS YOUR STORE FAILED TO HIT TARGET?" was the constant

Copyright © Tom Neath 2018
All Rights Reserved

question that Mr.G had to answer.

He gave the perfectly reasonable explanation that he had his regular staff away, but this did not stop the barrage of phone calls from engulfing the store. By the end of the first week the shop had fell drastically short of its weekly target and head office informed Mr.G by email, that in no uncertain terms, the following week's sales figures must significantly improve, or he would receive a written warning. (Notice that the threat was not made in person or even through a telephone conversation, but through a gutless email.)

If he were to receive this warning to partner his previous warning he acquired from the incident involving Mr.S's bike, then he would be just one warning away from being dismissed. Make no mistake, Mr.G was now a very worried man. The following week he tried desperately to get the sales through the till, and despite some success, the trend from the previous week continued and the sales figures were well below target. By the end of the second week, Mr.G had received his second warning and informed that if sales figures did not improve drastically, then he would incur the dreaded third warning, and dismissal would be on its way.

Upon our return to work, I swear that Mr.S and I had never seen Mr.G look so happy to see us!!! He looked like that he had the weight of the world on his shoulders. I asked him if his favourite sex shop had gone out of business!!! He told us what had happened over the previous two weeks and Mr.S wanted an immediate meeting with Mr.G, to which he agreed. What happened in the meeting was this - Mr.S informed Mr.G that he was mulling over a job offer from a rival company, but would have no hesitation in staying IF Mr.G quit the clowning around and started acting like the manager. Well, after the hellish experience of the last two weeks, Mr.G took just 0.01 of a second to agree to Mr.S's reasonable demands!!! From then on, despite not always hitting our daily target, the sales figures were certainly a lot healthier. With head office now off of Mr.G's back, he was very much a relieved man. From this point on Mr.G and Mr.S had a decent working relationship, and although they were never going to reach the status of best buddies, their work dialogue was often entwined with some social banter, and Mr.G would often provide biscuits for Mr.S's (now less frequent) cups of tea! But Mr.S firmly drew the line at accepting Mr.G's invitation in accompanying him on his once weekly visit to his favourite sex shop!!! It's just such a shame that their new found harmony would turn out to be in vain.

Copyright © Tom Neath 2018
All Rights Reserved

I enquired about the health of Mr.S's family member and his response was not one that I expected. A little startled, he replied;

"Pardon? Oh, um, yes he's fine thanks. Well on the road to recovery" and he then quickly changes the subject!

That was the last that myself and Mr.G heard on the subject. Now, I'm not making any accusations whatsoever, but could 'a very ill family member' have been a little plan concocted by Mr.S in an attempt to curb Mr.G's eccentric ways once and for all?! Oh come on Tom, pull yourself together.

Copyright © Tom Neath 2018
All Rights Reserved

TRIVIAL MATTERS

"Oh no, the zip makes a noise when the jacket is being done up!"

"I'm so worried that this £9.99 poncho will get creased if I put it in my bag"

"These socks are not the right shade of navy that I require, just what am I going to do?"

These are just some of the 'life stopping' issues that customers have grappled with down the years. A note to these customers - for goodness sake, WAKE UP!!! There are plenty more serious issues in life to think about. Forget about recession, greedy bankers, war and famine, as long as this next customer could make a decision on whether or not to purchase one of our travel sink plugs, then world order could continue!

It was summer 2006 and I approached a lady in her mid-twenties that was holding one of our travel sink plugs and asked if I could be of assistance? The lady replied that she had just popped in for one of our sink plugs, and asked if they were any good. I was just about to get in to my 'sink plug sales patter' when the lady fired another question at me.

"What's the specifications?"

Professionalism quickly flew out the window as I replied.

"SPECIFICATIONS?! IT'S A SMALL CIRCULAR PEICE OF RUBBER PRICED AT ONE POUND FIFTY!!! SO THERE ARE NO SPECIFICATIONS!"

Honesty soon bordered on rudeness as I continued.

"BUT WHAT I CAN TELL YOU IS THAT THE CUSTOMERS THAT WE HAVE SOLD PLUGS TO HAVE NEVER COME BACK TO COMPLAIN, BUT PERHAPS THAT IS BECAUSE THE PLUGS DO NOT WORK AND THE CUSTOMER HAS BEEN SUCKED DOWN THE PLUG HOLE, NEVER TO RETURN!!!"

The lady, through embarrassment or ignorance, did not respond to the comment and then said;

"Hmm, it's such a difficult decision, I just can't make my mind up. What do you think I should do?"

"Well, at one pound fifty, I say go mad and give it a go! LIVE FOR THE

Copyright © Tom Neath 2018
All Rights Reserved

MOMENT!!!" I replied.

After a further ten seconds of the lady waiting for me to make the decision for her, she said;

"I'll tell you what, I'll talk it over with my boyfriend tonight" and then puts the plug back into the stock. As the lady leaves the store I thought to myself that her boyfriend has an exciting night ahead of him!!!

I accept that it was not the ideal customer service, but I simply do not have time for people that worry about such trivial matters. If people concerned themselves with the important issues that life throws at us, then just maybe the world would be easier place to live. Amen.

These and all trivial matters were certainly put into perspective in my next story.

Copyright © Tom Neath 2018
All Rights Reserved

A TRIP DOWN MEMORY LANE

It was one quiet gloomy Monday in Autumn 2013, and Mr.S had just gone on his lunch break, leaving me to handle the tidal wave custom!!! (Ok, sarcasm may be the lowest form of wit, but it is certainly the funniest form of wit!)

My prayer for some custom was swiftly answered when an elderly husband and wife shuffled in to the shop. I greeted them to which the gentleman cheerfully repaid the compliment. His wife, walking stick in hand, was so breathless that I thought that she had just completed the Bristol marathon! I offered the lady a seat and she gratefully accepted. I asked the couple how I could be of assistance and the gentleman replied that early next year his good lady wife will be climbing Ben Nevis and needs to be kitted out. As I picked my jaw up of the floor, I was about to respond when the gentleman bellowed;

"I'm just joking son!!!"

I would like to say that I knew that the gentleman was joking all along but this is Broadmead after all! The gentleman continued;

"I would like to see your men's and women's lightweight waterproof clothing, I'll look at your men's range first please."

I took the gentleman over to the men's waterproof clothing and he now spoke in a quiet tone, somewhat anxious that his wife did not hear our conversation.

"Sorry about the bad joke" the gentleman continued, *"my darling wife will certainly not be climbing Ben Nevis next year, as she will not be here next year. The cancer will have got the better of her by then."*

The gentleman was overcome with sorrow, but noticing that his wife was looking in our direction he quickly put on a brave face, as he wanted to stay strong for his loved one. I offered my sympathy for the couple's terrible situation. The gentleman continued;

"The wife and I are childhood sweethearts, we grew up in Barnstaple and married in 1951. Due to my work we were relocated to Bristol in 1965 and have not been back to Barnstaple since. My wife would like to have one last.....'

I could see that the gentleman was getting emotional, so I discreetly offered him a tissue, he then continued;

".....one last look around Barnstaple. We have some wonderful memories and we

Copyright © Tom Neath 2018
All Rights Reserved

will be visiting all our old haunts. The wife is getting less mobile as each week goes by and some day's the pain gets too much for her. I suppose that I should be encouraging her to rest at home, but this is her dying wish."

The gentleman did a much better job at putting on a brave face than I did, as by this point I had to wipe away a tear. I do not usually get too emotionally involved with customers, but this was a unique situation, right? The gentleman's wife was looking anxiously over at us, so I knew that I had to quickly compose myself, so that I could effectively assist in clothing the couple out for their poignant trip down memory lane.

This may sound daft, but I didn't want the couple to be apart from each other any longer than necessary, so I invited the gentleman to re-join his wife and I brought over a selection of men's and ladies waterproof garments. As the couple were trying on the garments, I politely excused myself, and I shortly returned with a cup of tea for the couple. They were overjoyed at my little act of kindness.

"Do you do bacon rolls as well?!" the gentleman then quipped

I guess that I could be accused of showing customer favouritism, but what the heck! How many customers do you think that I have served in my time that have only a matter of months left with their loved ones?

While the couple were trying on the selection of garments, they were talking about their time in Barnstaple - where they met, where they used to go dancing and where the gentleman made his marriage proposal. Their favourite past time was to go the picture house, the Gaumont as it was known then, though not always to watch the film, the gentleman commented as he winked at me!!! Whatever did he mean?! I didn't go too much into the technical specifications of the waterproof clothing that the couple were trying on, as they had more pressing issues to contend with. I simply assured them that the garments were absolutely fine for their requirements of keeping dry if the good old British weather takes a turn for the worse. The couple selected the garments that they would like to purchase, and I took the garments to the cash desk and started scanning the items through the till. As I was doing this, I overheard the gentleman ask his wife if she wanted him to fetch her wheelchair from the car.

"While the cancer stays away from my legs, I will be clocking up their mileage" she replied.

I thought what a courageous response in not letting this terrible illness affect the

Copyright © Tom Neath 2018
All Rights Reserved

time that that she has left.

As the couple were getting themselves together, a suited customer brashly enters the store and demands that I help him with some walking socks 'right this instance!' I politely told the customer that I was currently serving, so pointed him in the direction of the sock department, and said that I would be with him shortly. A sigh and sulky look proceeded from the customer as he trudged off to look at the socks. The couple made their way to the cash desk, I processed their payment and handed the gentleman their garments. Without knowing the exact words to use when someone only has a matter of months left to live, I simply said;

"I hope that Barnstaple is still as magical for you as it was all those years ago."

The gentleman winked at me, and the couple shuffled out of the shop, ready to relive some happy memories.

As I gathered up the cups that the couple had been drinking from, I spotted a note and three pound coins. The note read 'thank you for your help and the tea young man, now have a drink on us'. Now, with the trauma that they were going through, I was touched by such a nice thought.

"I'M STILL WAITING!" barked out the suited customer who was holding a pair of socks. I was just about to respond when he demanded to know what was so special about the socks that he had in hand. With such a striking contrast between this customer and the elderly couple so highly evident, I was struggling to keep my cool.

"SPECIAL?! They are just a pair of socks! But I'll give you a definition of special - special is having a loving relationship for over fifty years, where you would go to the end of the earth to ensure your partners happiness - that's special, sir."

At this point Mr.S had returned from a break, so I asked him to take over and serve the customer, while I took a much needed breather in the staff room. I dare say that the customer would have felt inclined to lodge a complaint against me, but after a feeling of sadness at the couple's story, yet indulging in a sense of pride that I was able to assist a couple in their most important trip of their lives, I can honestly say that I couldn't give two hoots if the customer did complain about me.

Copyright © Tom Neath 2018
All Rights Reserved

THE FINAL THROW OF THE DICE

In Spring 2014, Broadmead had witnessed no fewer than twenty shops close down, due to the ugly effects from the recession. Despite my shop putting up a decent fight against the recession, the first quarter of 2014 had seen the company record its lowest customer footfall figures and more importantly, its lowest ever sales figures. In a nutshell, the company was struggling to stay afloat. Head office could not understand why the spring and extra 20 per cent sales were failing to have the desired effect. Well, the answer was simple - the sales are losing their pulling power. The sales are a tool used by the shops to draw customers in, and up until very recently has always been successful. But when pretty much all the shops are having sales all year round, they become standard, and therefore they lose their unique ability in being able to attract customers in to the shop. But the company's website, which stocks exactly the same items as the shops, was recording good sales figures. Why? Because you could purchase items from the company's website for just two thirds of the shop price!!! Even with the postage and packaging cost, the customer was still making a heck of a saving. Why would a customer pay the full shop price, when they can get it cheaper online?! But head office refused to acknowledge this critical fact, and constantly berated the shops for being out performed by the website. Despite the good sales figures from the company's website, it was not enough to safeguard the long term future of the company and we knew that a major upturn in sales was needed otherwise the local job centre would be gaining some new recruits!

Late one afternoon the shop received an email from the owner of the company requesting that all staff dress up in the shop's clothing and/or equipment from the start of the following day. This was an idea designed to catch the eye of passers-by, and attract them in to the shop. Could this latest bout of eccentricity from the company owner turn out to be the idea that prevents the company from going bust? With our jobs on the line, myself, Mr.G, Mr.S and the part-time member of staff were prepared to give it a go.

The following day we all arrived an hour before being open for trade so we could sort our costumes out. The first suggestion of what to wear came from Mr.G.

"Why don't we all wear one of the shops vibrant coloured, full length waterproof

Copyright © Tom Neath 2018
All Rights Reserved

garments and form a camping shop music quartet called THE FUNKY PONCHOS!!!"

After composing myself from a fit of laughter, I reminded Mr.G that the email had also requested that we all dressed different from one another. After ten minutes of deliberation I put on a beige shirt, pair of beige shorts, knee length socks, wide brim hat, hung a compass around my neck and became 'SAFARI MAN!'

Mr.G adopted his ski man outfit previously described at the start of the book.

The most creative award went to Mr.S as he pulled out a mummy shaped sleeping bag from the faulty stock box, cut holes out for his arms and legs and pulled the sleeping bag over himself, with his face poking through the top of the sleeping bag! As it was a high warmth rated sleeping bag, he was wearing just boxer shorts and socks on underneath, yet how he did not sweat to death, I'll never know! The part-time member of staff put on a waterproof jacket and over trousers, a day sack and hung a map case around his neck and became RAMBLER MAN! The new look was complete folks!

After some very stressful months, this idea had injected a bit of light relief in to the shop and we were optimistic that this idea could work and we could get some much needed money through the till. Mr.G opened up the shop - bring on the customers! Well folks, by one o clock the shop had made the grand total of £53.86! Definitely not the sales figures that we had hoped for. Mr.G sent the company owner the disheartening news and asked if he wanted us to continue with the costumes. 'Yes continue!' was the short and shrift response! Yes sir, right away sir! Another hour with just one low value purchase had passed by when, via the shop security radio, we heard security guards passing animated messages back and forth. The two policemen entered the shop and we were under strict instruction to leave the shop right away! As we were being escorted out of the shop - still in costume - we were informed by the policemen that the whole of the Broadmead shopping centre was being evacuated due to a bomb scare! Mr.G locked up the shop and we were ushered five hundred yards down the road to where staff from the other shops had assembled. Mr.G, using his mobile phone, informed the company owner about the situation and he informed us to stay near the shop in case we get the all clear to resume trading. So, there we were - four odd balls stuck in our outrageous clothing, and sleeping bag - amongst the more suitably dressed retail staff from Broadmead! It was a picture I can tell you!!! We couldn't even go into a budget price clothing

Copyright © Tom Neath 2018
All Rights Reserved

store to purchase some emergency clothing because of the Broadmead lock down! What a predicament folks.

Such quips from people were;

"Where are you from?"

"Have you been separated from your carer?"

"Are you a very bad 'The Village People' tribute act?"

We explained the surreal situation and then something odd happened - people started to ask us about the stock that we were so elegantly modelling and were showing a genuine interest in making some purchases! But we could not do a damn thing to get the sales through the till because of the Broadmead lockdown! AAAAAAGH!!!

Four o'clock had arrived and there was no sign of being able to resume trading and we were advised by police that we were better off going home and listen out for updates with regards to being able to resume trade the following day. Again Mr.G informed the company owner of this and he begrudgingly agreed with the advice of the police. We were free to go home early, brilliant! Mr.S tried to reason with the nearby policeman that he needed to go back into the shop to retrieve his bike, but draped head to toe in a sleeping bag, how seriously do you think that the policeman took him?! Mr.S had to join myself, Mr.G and the part-time member of staff in using the bus service by means of getting home. Then we stopped and thought 'is that wise?' For fear of insults and even the dark possibility of being set upon by a gang of thugs, we decided that the best solution to our predicament was to club together and book a taxi to get us safely home. A sniggering taxi driver would be a lot easier to take over a barrage of bruises! Mr.G lived the furthest away, so he would be last to be dropped off. As each of us were dropped off at our destination Mr.G reminded us not to forget to bring our costumes back in to work the following day, as they are the company's property. Oh, and there was me thinking that we could wear the costumes Saturday night out on the town!!!

Seriously though, after such a surreal day we were hardly likely to forget to bring the costumes back in to the shop! That night the local news announced that the bomb scare was over and the shops were given the green light to open as normal, the following the day.

The following day Mr.G emailed the owner of the company asking if he wanted

Copyright © Tom Neath 2018
All Rights Reserved

us to continue with the costumes, which oddly, he received no reply. So not wanting to take a chance on the previous day's events occurring again, we took the decision to revert back to our usual staff uniform. Five minutes before we were due to open for trade, some customers had assembled outside the shop! Excellent! We opened up the shop early to seize the opportunity to gain some much needed sales, and these customers were the people that had been inquiring about our costumes during the bomb scare. In the first hour we had made over £400!!! For the remainder of the morning there was a steady flow of custom and by midday we had hit the £800 mark! Happy days! It felt like that the tide was finally turning and that the company was coming out of intensive care and hopefully go on to make a full recovery. Then we received an email from the owner of the company that brought our worlds crashing down.

Copyright © Tom Neath 2018
All Rights Reserved

IT'S GOODNIGHT FROM HIM

There are very few problems that life throws at us that cannot be dealt with by a doctor, a lawyer or a hitman! Unfortunately for myself, Mr.G, Mr.S and the part-time member of staff, one of these very few problems had been bowled at us by the owner of the company. Mentioned at the end of the previous chapter, the email informed us that the company owner could no longer afford to run the business and had agreed to sell the company to a rival camping and outdoor clothing company. The email also stated that it was with regret that the long term employment of staff could not be guaranteed, and finished up by thanking us for our hard work down the years. (Yet again, bad news delivered in the gutless form of an email.)

Another email was shortly received stating that a letter with more information would be sent out to each member of staff in due course. It was just as well, as we were running low on toilet paper!!!

My feelings consisted of sadness, anger and betrayal. Sadness, because I enjoy my work and I have been quite lucky in the fact that I have worked with people that I have had a rapport with. (You can choose your friends but you can't choose your work colleagues.) I felt anger that the company owner did not inform us earlier of his plans. Let's face it, a deal to sell the company must have been in the pipeline for a couple of months, at least. The shop staff have kept him in a life of luxury down the years and he repays us by selling up, making a nice few quid and leaving us with the very real possibility of being unemployed. Finally, I felt betrayed, because the owner had agreed to sell the company to a rival business. Now, the rival business is a much bigger fish in the camping and outdoor clothing pond and it did not take a genius to realise what was going to happen. This was the ideal opportunity for the rival business to rid itself of some of the competition, then with the view to close down the shops it has just purchased and leave myself and others without a job. Bastards.

With this in mind, our thoughts and efforts were not anymore focused on sales, but now on finding a new job. Not an easy task in the financial climate, but by the end of the week each member of staff had at least one interview for alternative work lined up. We had heard whispers regarding how this new company treated its staff, and let's just say, it was not complimentary. By the end of the following week the

Copyright © Tom Neath 2018
All Rights Reserved

sale of the company was complete and our humbly priced stock was transferred to the previously mentioned website store, which was going to continue to trade. As this was taking place, the new company's stock was brought in to store along with their hard line procedures.

As the new company did not want to pay out redundancy money to their recently gained recruits, they wasted no time implementing these hard line procedures in the hope of pushing us closer to the exit door and that we would leave on our own free will.

With the part-time member of staff leaving with immediate effect due to university commitments, this left myself, Mr.G and Mr.S waiting to hear the outcomes from our recent interviews. It must have been written in the stars, because just the following day we had been given the news that our job applications had been successful. It was official - Mr.G, Mr.S and I, with a combined retail experience of over fifty years, were leaving the shop. It was the end of an era.

Copyright © Tom Neath 2018
All Rights Reserved

MY LAST SALE

'And now, the end is near and so I face my final curtain.'

Ok, I'll put the microphone down now folks!!! Mr.G, Mr.S and I had handed in a week's notice and we were scheduled to leave on the same day. I'll be honest, knowing that the sales made in my last week would be lining the pockets of these new bastard company owners, it was difficult to muster the enthusiasm to sell to the customers. However, it was hardly the customer's fault the way events turned out the way that they did, so I remained professional and helpful to the customers and their requests.

The Area Manager from the new company had been ever present in store since the sale was confirmed, to oversee the transition, and I had done very well to bite my tongue and keep my cool with this very unreasonable guy. My tongue biting and coolness was to fly out of the window on my last day!!!

One the new company's procedures was that they demanded that with every sale over £10, the customer MUST be sold an additional half price item which would be no more than the cost of £5. These glamorous additional items consisted of a compact umbrella, a water bottle and a wind up torch. If you did not hit your weekly target for additional item sales, then you would receive a warning. I repeat - bastards.

With staff worried about picking up these warnings, I can imagine staff getting quite desperate and/or aggressive in trying to sell these additional items - hardly the required ingredients for decent customer service now is it?!

Also, how many times have you been into a shop and been asked by the till assistant *'would you like a half price such and such or would you like some chocolate for a pound?'* NO! Because if I wanted it, I would ask for it!!!

Despite taking a strong dislike to this procedure, I followed orders, but put in the bare minimum of effort in selling these additional items. If they wanted to sack me then fine, I have another job to go into!

It had just gone midday and I was serving a gentleman who was interested in the range of the new £300 waterproof jackets now being stocked. As I was going through the sales patter, the gentleman tried on a selection of these top end jackets

Copyright © Tom Neath 2018
All Rights Reserved

and after fifteen minutes he chose a jacket to purchase. BINGO! I was going out with a bang. In the excitement of such a terrific sale I forgot to offer the gentleman an additional sale, but what the heck, I had just put a mammoth sized purchase through the till. The gentleman thanked me for my service, left the shop and I tidied up the jackets that the gentleman had tried on. As I was doing this the Area Manager approached me and said;

"Excuse me?"

"Yes?" I replied, fully expecting a well done for such a fine sale.

"You did not offer the customer an additional sale, can you tell me why?" The Area Manager asked. I was stunned. *"Come on, I want an explanation!"*

Right oh matey, time for my reply!

"I have just sold the shop's most expensive jacket, making £300, and you are stood here, quizzing me on why I have not sold the customer a damn additional sale?! YOU ARE TAKING THE PISS!!!"

Well, that was the final straw folks, as I brought forward my leaving to right there and then! Mr.G and Mr.S, who were also at the end of their tether with the Area Manager, accompanied myself in leaving at that moment too! The three musketeers had left the building! I was touched at such an act of unity by the two people that I had shared the same piece of carpet with for the last fifteen years. As previously mentioned, this new company had an agenda to force us out of the doors and although Mr.G, Mr.S and I had made it nice and easy for them, we took a greater pleasure knowing that we would not be making a penny more for those bastards.

As I was waiting on the bus stop for my home commute, I thought to myself why have I done this job for the last fifteen years all for it to end so very bitterly? Then I remembered the feelings that I experienced from helping the elderly couple that were going back to Barnstaple - that's why I have done this job for the last fifteen years.

This was not the last time that Mr.G, Mr.S and I would grace each other with our presence, as we had arranged to go out for a farewell meal on the same night. Well why not, the bakery lets you eat-in these days and stays open late!!! I'm joking of course, we went to a well-known American themed restaurant.

Myself and Mr.S arrived at the same time and were shown to our table by the waiter. Five minutes later Mr.G arrives holding a large carrier bag and wearing a ski helmet!!! At this point Mr.S asked the waiter for a double brandy!

Copyright © Tom Neath 2018
All Rights Reserved

Mr.G joined us at the table and pulled out two ski helmets from the carrier bag for myself and Mr.S to wear, so now it was my turn to order a double brandy! We begrudgingly decided to wear the helmets and yes, we did get some funny looks from the waiting staff and diners alike, but what the heck, it was the last time that we would be together. During our meal we discussed our new career paths - Mr.S was joining a well-known bicycle company and Mr.G was joining a well-known paint company. So Mr.G's new sales one liner is going to be *'I used to sell overcoats, now I sell undercoats!'* Brilliant.

So, what new work venture lies in wait for myself? Well you will just have to read my next book of stories to find out!

As we left the restaurant we shook hands, wished each other luck for the future and went our separate ways.

With my hands in my pockets, I walked into the cold calm night thinking about all these stories that I have relayed to you. I am sure that not everyone will like or agree with my opinions, thoughts and actions, but at the end of the day folks, we are all different and that's what makes the world go round.

'Yes, I did it, my way.'

Copyright © Tom Neath 2018
All Rights Reserved

23337647R00056

Printed in Poland
by Amazon Fulfillment
Poland Sp. z o.o., Wrocław